Brian Keaney was born in London where he still lives. His parents were Irish and he learned story-telling from his mother. When he was a child, she told him stories while she worked and he followed her around the house, listening eagerly to every word. He decided to become a writer while he was still at school but it turned out to be more difficult than he expected and he is still learning. Most days he is to be found in his study, writing on his computer, but he spends a part of every summer in the West of Ireland, a place where he dreams of living all the time.

'Brian Keaney's writing is spare and taut and there is never a word out of place or one that doesn't ring true.'
Anthony Masters,
Times Educational Supplement

BITTER FRUIT

BRIAN KEANEY

 ORCHARD BOOKS

To Kathleen

ORCHARD BOOKS
96 Leonard Street, London EC2A 4XD
Orchard Books Australia
14 Mars Road, Lane Cove, NSW 2066
A paperback original
ISBN 1 84121 005 6
First published in Great Britain in 1999
© Brian Keaney 1999
The right of Brian Keaney to be identified as the author
of this work has been asserted by him in accordance with
the Copyright, Designs and Patents Act, 1988
A CIP catalogue record for this book is available
from the British Library.
Printed and bound in Great Britain

CHAPTER ONE

'This is what life is supposed to be like,' Rebecca said to herself. It was Friday night and it was late. Outside the weather was cold. Autumn was turning into winter and you could hear the wind blowing in sudden fierce gusts. But in Zoe's room at the top of the house it was warm and cosy. There was no one in the house but Rebecca, Hannah and Zoe. They were sitting in the soft light of candles that Zoe had stuck into empty wine bottles. Pools of shadow lay in the corners, giving the room the air of a cave. Candle wax had dripped down the sides of the wine bottles, making Rebecca think of stalactites. It was as if the three girls had discovered their own little hideaway from the outside world, a place where no one could reach them.

Zoe, who had been bending over the CD player, turned round. 'This is such a brilliant album,' she told them. 'You'll love it.'

Zoe was always right about stuff like that. She had the best albums before anyone else. She knew the right places to buy clothes, the places that were fashionable and those that weren't. Rebecca envied her. She could go where she liked. Her parents didn't make detailed enquiries every time she went outside the door. They were cool. Tonight they had gone to a party somewhere and they weren't coming back at all. They had left Zoe in charge. There was no chance of Rebecca's parents ever behaving like that. Especially her dad. He regarded Zoe's parents as highly irresponsible.

'Who wants another drink?' Zoe enquired. She stood in the middle of the room with a bottle of whisky in one hand and a bottle of Coca-Cola in the other. She was tall and slim with long dark hair. She looked older than fourteen.

Rebecca hadn't finished her drink but she gulped it down.

'Won't your parents notice that the whisky's gone?' Rebecca asked.

'I'll just deny everything,' Zoe said. 'Stonewall them. It always works.'

Rebecca couldn't imagine it working with her parents.

Zoe filled up their glasses.

'I think I'm getting to like the taste of whisky,' Hannah said, giggling. Hannah was the youngest of the three of them, which made it particularly annoying that she was generally allowed out later than Rebecca. Her parents weren't as liberal as Zoe's but she could get around them when she wanted to. For instance, she was staying at Zoe's tonight.

That wasn't an option for Rebecca. 'I don't think she's a particularly good influence on you,' that was what Carol, her mother, said, whenever Rebecca mentioned Zoe's name. Richard, her father, put it more strongly: 'That girl is totally out of control,' he insisted when Zoe got her eyebrow pierced.

'I think it looks nice,' Rebecca told him.

'Nice!' he said, in a tone of outrage. 'Well you needn't

think you're getting it done.'

'I didn't say I was, did I?' Rebecca replied. As a matter of fact she had come very close to getting it done at the same time as Zoe.

'Go on!' Zoe had urged her. 'He can't say anything once it's done, can he?'

But she knew it was pointless. He would have made her take it out.

'What do her teachers say about her?' Carol asked.

Rebecca had shrugged. It was the kind of stupid question her parents were always asking.

'But do they let her wear that ring through her eyebrow to school?' Carol continued.

Rebecca sighed. 'She takes it out for school.'

'I should think so too,' Richard said. 'Someone needs to exercise some control over that girl.'

Zoe, the girl over whom someone needed to exercise some control, stood beside Rebecca holding out the whisky bottle like a waitress. 'A drop of the hard stuff?' she asked.

'Why not?' Rebecca said. The alcohol that she had already consumed was beginning to affect her in a way that was really rather pleasant. She felt happy. It was good to have good friends.

Zoe poured out a generous measure of whisky and added plenty of Coca-Cola. Then, as if she had read Rebecca's mind, she raised her glass and said, rather theatrically, 'To friendship.'

Rebecca and Hannah raised their own glasses. 'To friendship,' they chorused.

You needed friends if you lived in a place like Beckerton,

that was Rebecca's opinion. It was total suburbia. Nothing had ever happened there. Nothing was ever going to happen here. You could walk down the street and in every house the same thing was going on: people were watching TV screens, putting the cat out and going to bed early.

'There must be something that happens to people when they get to a certain age,' Rebecca said, 'something in the genes, maybe, that makes them want to go to bed early, every night.'

'I don't think my parents have got that gene,' Zoe said.

'It must have missed them,' Rebecca agreed.

'They're some sort of mutation,' Zoe said, giggling.

That made them all laugh. It wasn't especially funny but they were in the mood for laughter. It felt good to laugh. Hannah was laughing so much her eyes were watering.

Zoe went over to her dressing-table. She opened one of the drawers and rummaged around inside it. Then she brought something out and held it up with a flourish of triumph. 'Look what Zoe's got,' she said.

'What is it?' Rebecca asked.

'Dope,' she said.

'Oh, wow!' Hannah said. 'Well done, Zoe!'

Rebecca had not smoked any dope before, but she was keen to try it. Hannah made out that she had smoked it a few times, though Rebecca doubted whether this was true. Zoe certainly had smoked it before and what's more she knew how to score it for herself.

'Where did you get it?' Rebecca asked.

'I have my connections,' Zoe said, enigmatically. She sat down again. 'Time to skin up.' She produced a packet of cigarettes and some rolling papers from her pocket and began to construct a joint. Rebecca watched her enviously.

The joint took a little while to roll and it wasn't exactly a work of art. Clearly, Zoe wasn't as expert at this as she liked to make out. When she had finally finished she put it between her lips and lit the end. The paper flared up then settled down to a red glow as she drew in the smoke.

'Not bad,' said Zoe, blowing out the smoke in a stream. 'Not bad at all.' She passed the joint to Rebecca.

Rebecca had smoked cigarettes before, though she didn't particularly enjoy them, but this was nothing like a cigarette. The smoke that filled her lungs when she inhaled was fiercely hot. She fought the urge to cough but it was too strong for her.

Zoe looked superior. 'Draw it in gently,' she told Rebecca. 'Don't try and take it all down at once.'

Rebecca's eyes were watering. She handed the joint to Hannah who took it and inhaled carefully without coughing.

'I didn't expect it to be so harsh,' Rebecca said, apologetically.

'It's like that for everyone the first time they try it,' Zoe told her.

The joint went round again and this time Rebecca managed to hold the smoke in her lungs for a little while before blowing it out again. She waited for some sort of reaction. She wasn't sure exactly what she was supposed to feel, but for some reason it didn't seem to be affecting her at all.

'Are you starting to feel mellow?' Zoe asked. This was one of her favourite expressions.

'Mmm!' said Hannah. Her eyes were closed and she had a smile on her face.

'How about you, Beck?' Zoe asked.

'Definitely,' Rebecca said, but she wasn't really. Nothing seemed to be happening at all. She was disappointed but she didn't say anything. Instead, she sat back and listened to the music, trying to smile like Hannah had.

Zoe was certainly right about the album. It was incredible. There seemed to be layers and layers of sound. Sometimes they merged together and then at other times they separated. It was like a sea of sound and you could swim around inside it, sometimes going right underneath and then at other times coming up to the surface.

'Are you OK, Beck?' Zoe asked.

'What?'

'Are you OK?'

'Yeah.'

'I just thought you looked a bit weird.'

'I'm fine.'

That was slightly annoying, Zoe asking her if she was OK. It was like putting her in her place, making it clear that Zoe was the most experienced, at least that was how it seemed to Rebecca. As if Zoe thought she couldn't handle it.

Rebecca started listening to the music again. She wanted to lose herself in that sea of sound but for some reason she couldn't do it. She had a distinct feeling that something was wrong. It was like swimming in a warm blue sea and then encountering a cold current, a current that came from some-where deep beneath the surface.

Rebecca sat up. Thoughts seemed to be going on in her

head of their own accord, as if she was not really in control of them. She needed to get a grip on things. Something was definitely happening and she wasn't at all sure that she liked it. She needed to concentrate. She wished she had not drunk quite so much whisky.

She began to feel incredibly tired. Her arms and legs felt like they were made of melting chocolate. She had an almost overwhelming urge to just lie down on the floor, close her eyes and go to sleep. But she couldn't do that because she was also beginning to feel a little bit dizzy. She closed her eyes. That was a terrible mistake. Everything immediately started going round and round. It was a horrible sensation and it was getting stronger. She realised with dismay that there was a possibility she might be sick at any moment. She struggled against the feeling of nausea, but it was no good.

She got to her feet with difficulty and stood there, unsteadily. 'I'm just going to the loo,' was what she meant to say but it came out as 'Imussgunnaloo.'

The other two giggled. 'What did you say?' Zoe asked.

Rebecca didn't bother to repeat herself. She now felt certain that something very unpleasant was going to happen to her at any moment. She had to get to the bathroom in a hurry. She plunged across the room, seized the door handle and pulled it open, then ran down the stairs to the bathroom on the floor below. She pushed open the door and was immediately sick into the toilet bowl.

It was horrible, but afterwards she felt a little better. She flushed the toilet and rinsed her mouth with mouthwash. She felt weak and her head hurt. It was time to go home, she decided.

'Are you OK?' Zoe said. She was waiting outside.

'I was sick.'

'I heard you.'

There didn't seem to be much else to say. Rebecca felt miserable, as if she had just taken an exam in being cool and failed.

'Do you want a drink of water?'

'Thanks.'

Zoe went downstairs and came back a minute later with a glass of water. Rebecca sat on the stairs and sipped it. It tasted very cold and made her shiver.

'There was a message on the answerphone downstairs,' Zoe said. 'It was from your dad.'

'Oh God!' Rebecca moaned. 'That's all I need.' She stood up shakily. 'I'd better listen to it.'

The two girls went downstairs into the kitchen and Zoe switched on the answerphone.

'This is Richard Healy, Rebecca's father,' the message began. 'It's twelve o'clock on Friday night.' Rebecca hadn't realised it was so late. She looked at her watch. It was now twelve-thirty.

'I'm looking for Rebecca,' her father continued. 'I'm not sure where she's gone but she ought to be back by now. If she is there, or if there is anyone there who knows where she is, perhaps you could give me a ring back.'

He sounded cross.

'I'd better go home,' Rebecca said.

'Are you sure you're all right?'

'I'm fine.'

At that moment the doorbell rang. Whoever was ringing it

12

meant business. They let it ring long and hard before they took their finger off.

'Guess who?' Rebecca said.

'Your dad?'

'Bound to be.'

'Shall I answer?'

'I'll do it,' Rebecca said.

'Don't bring him upstairs,' Zoe said. 'He'll smell the smoke.'

'Don't worry, I won't.'

The doorbell rang again. Rebecca waited for Zoe to scamper upstairs, then she went to the front door and opened it. The cold night air came rushing in. Her father stood framed in the doorway. 'So you are here!' he said, angrily.

She couldn't think of anything to say to that.

'Have you any idea what time it is?' he demanded.

'I was just going.'

'Just going!' He spat the words back at her. 'You should have been home an hour ago.'

'I'm sorry. I didn't notice the time.'

'Didn't notice the time! What kind of a stupid thing to say is that?'

Rebecca said nothing.

'Why didn't you answer the telephone?'

'You can't hear it in Zoe's room.'

'Well you ought to be able to hear it!'

'Sorry.'

'Sorry isn't good enough. Do you think I haven't got better things to do than to drive around in the middle of the night scouring Beckerton for you?'

'I don't know.'

'What's that supposed to mean?' He looked as if he suspected her of trying to be clever.

'Nothing. I mean, I'm sorry.'

'Oh for God's sake! Just go and get your coat. And hurry up. It's freezing out here.'

She went back upstairs and got her coat. Hannah and Zoe were looking sympathetic. 'Is he very angry?' Zoe said.

Rebecca nodded. She didn't feel like going into detail. 'See you later,' she said. She put on her coat, waved feebly then went downstairs. She felt completely humiliated, as if she was about four years old and her father had come to collect her from a birthday party.

They drove home in silence but Rebecca knew that he was saving it up for when they got indoors. Well he could say what he wanted. She didn't care. It was her life. She was entitled to live it the way she wanted to.

When she got indoors, her mother was in the kitchen in her dressing-gown and slippers, making a cup of tea.

'She was round at Zoe's then?' she said to Richard.

'Of course she was,' he replied. He made it sound like a criminal offence.

'Rebecca darling, why didn't you answer the telephone?' Carol asked.

'I didn't hear it.'

'Now listen to me,' Richard said. 'I want to make one thing clear. I am not prepared to put up with this sort of behaviour.'

'What sort of behaviour?' Rebecca said.

'Staying out all night.'

'I haven't been staying out all night,' she objected.

'Oh I see, you were just on your way home when I called.'

'Yes I was as a matter of fact.'

'That's very likely.'

'It's the truth.'

'The point is, Rebecca, that you can't just disappear without telling anyone where you're going.'

Rebecca suddenly felt totally fed up with the whole thing. They were so boring, both of them, her mother in that dreadful towelling dressing-gown that she had had for years and her father standing there talking to her as if she had no mind of her own. 'Why?' she said.

Her father looked startled. 'What sort of a question is that meant to be?' he demanded.

'Why do I have to tell you where I'm going all the time?'

He opened his mouth to speak, then closed it again. Finally he said, 'Because I'm your father.' It sounded pathetic.

'So?'

She could tell by his face that she had really infuriated him now. 'So!' he repeated. He turned to Carol. 'For God's sake, what kind of an idiot is she?'

'I'm not an idiot,' she said. It was her turn to be angry now. Just because he couldn't think of an answer he called her an idiot.

'Well you behave like one! You're nothing but trouble.'

Rebecca's head was throbbing and she was completely exhausted.

'What's the matter with you?' Richard said, suddenly. 'You look terrible.' He sniffed. 'You smell of smoke. What have you been up to?'

'I haven't been up to anything,' Rebecca protested. But she didn't sound very convincing.

'That's the last time you go round to Zoe's house,' Richard said. He looked her straight in the eye. She could tell that he meant it.

At that moment she felt nothing but contempt for him. He was such a pain! 'I hate you!' she said. That stopped him in his tracks! She waited for one second, just to savour the look on his face. Then she turned round and went upstairs to her room. She slammed the door behind her. Now he knew how it felt.

CHAPTER TWO

'Wake up, Rebecca. I've brought you a cup of tea, though you don't really deserve it.' It was her mother. Rebecca opened her eyes and then quickly shut them again. The light hurt.

'Come on, Rebecca. It's afternoon. You can't lie in bed all day.'

'I'm awake,' Rebecca moaned.

'Well stay awake. No going back to sleep.'

'OK.'

'I want you to get up and tidy this bedroom. It's a disgrace.'

'OK.' It was all she could manage to say in reply.

'Don't let that tea go cold,' Carol said, going out of the room.

Rebecca felt terrible. So this was what a hangover was like. Her head felt like there was a huge metal ball that rolled around inside it, every time she moved. Her mouth felt disgusting, 'like a camel's armpit', to use one of Zoe's phrases.

Very carefully, she sat up in bed. The metal ball rolled thunderously to the front of her head. She picked up the tea and drank it greedily, thinking over the events of the night before.

It had been worth it, she decided, even though she felt so excruciatingly awful. It had been worth it to do something a bit daring, to live a little. That was something her dad would never understand. For him every day was more or less the same: go to work, come home, go to bed, get up, go to work and on and on. But for Rebecca things were going to be different. Every day could be different. She was on a journey of discovery.

But she did feel terrible. She finished the tea, lay back and closed her eyes. She wondered whether Zoe and Hannah were up yet. Probably not. Lucky things. They could do what they liked.

'Are you getting up, Rebecca?' Carol called.

'Yes, Mum.'

Rebecca got out from underneath the duvet and sat on the edge of the bed. Even that felt like a major effort. She looked critically around her room. It was a bit of a mess. There were dirty clothes all over the floor, as well as magazines, school books, the remains of a bowl of cornflakes and a couple of damp bath towels. She didn't feel much like tidying it up.

For some reason she could never get her room to look the way that she wanted. It always looked to her like a little girl's bedroom. No matter what she did, it didn't compare with Zoe's attic room. There was no atmosphere. She had put up posters, hung things from the ceiling, even tried using candles instead of the electric light, much to her mother's dismay, but somehow it was not the same. It would always be a room in her parent's house, never her own space.

She needed something to eat, she decided. There was a hole in her stomach that was crying out to be filled. She pulled on her clothes and went into the kitchen to find something to eat.

'You look in good shape,' Carol said.

'I'm all right.'

'Your voice sounds husky.'

'I think I'm getting a cold.'

'Hmm,' Carol said. She didn't sound terribly impressed.

Rebecca got herself some cereal. But after eating a couple of spoonfuls she pushed it away.

'What's the matter with it?' Carol asked.

'I just don't feel hungry.'

The truth was that eating immediately made her feel sick all over again but she couldn't tell her mother that.

'It's a waste of good food.'

'I'm sorry.'

Carol looked frustrated. 'I don't know what's the matter with you nowadays,' she told Rebecca.

'There's nothing the matter with me.'

'You were extremely unpleasant to your dad last night.'

'He was unpleasant to me, first.'

Carol sighed. 'It doesn't seem to be any use talking to you,' she said.

'Where is he now, anyway?' Rebecca asked.

'He's working today.'

Rebecca's father worked for a company that made parts for computers. He was a middle manager, which just about suited him in Rebecca's opinion – a middle manager from suburbia. More and more often these days he had to work at weekends. It was something her mother had often complained about. Rebecca had no idea what she wanted to be when she was grown up, but she was pretty sure of one thing: she was not going to be a little cog in a big machine, like her father.

'I think you'd better get on with tidying your bedroom,' Carol said. 'It's about time you did something useful.'

It was a day of slow-motion. Everything Rebecca did seemed to take an enormous amount of effort. Just bending down to pick something up off the floor was hard work. Every now and again she got a touch of that spinning sensation that she had experienced the night before, nothing serious, but enough to make her hold her head in her hands and moan to herself.

She made some progress with her room. She got things picked up off the floor, the dirty clothes in the laundry basket, the others hung up in the wardrobe. She put her school books away and took the bowl with the dried up corn-flakes out into the kitchen. It was a definite improvement, though there was still a lot to do. She decided to take a little rest.

The phone rang. Rebecca picked up the extension in her room. It was Zoe.

'How are you feeling?' she asked.

'Rough,' Rebecca told her.

'What did your dad say?'

'The usual. What did you do after I left?'

'Oh, you know, carried on till we crashed out.'

'Is Hannah still there?'

'Yeah.'

Rebecca felt a stab of envy. They were still enjoying them-selves while she was tidying her bedroom.

'Why don't you come over this afternoon?'

'I'm not allowed.'

'Can't you talk your parents round?'

'I'll try,' Rebecca said without much hope.

'OK. See you later.'

'Right.'

Carol poked her head around the door. 'What's happening about this room?' she asked.

'I'm tidying it,' Rebecca replied.

'Well you're not making very much progress. Who was that on the telephone?'

'Zoe. She wants me to go round there this afternoon. Can I, when I've finished my room?'

Carol shook her head. 'Absolutely not. You heard what your father said last night.'

'Oh, Mum!'

'I'm not interested,' Carol said. 'Now how about finishing this room?'

The day wore on but it did not get much easier. Carol was unrelenting. She made sure Rebecca finished her bedroom and she was unsympathetic when Rebecca told her she had a headache. 'You wouldn't have a headache if you went to bed on time,' was all she said.

Rebecca felt totally drained of energy. She wasn't looking forward to her dad coming home. She didn't feel up to any more arguments. So she was relieved when Carol said that he wouldn't be back for dinner. 'He's meeting someone after work,' she told Rebecca.

'He's always working,' Rebecca said.

'Money doesn't grow on trees, Rebecca,' Carol said crossly.

'I know that,' Rebecca said.

Her mother was not usually so sharp with her. It was normally her father who laid down the law. But this evening her mum seemed especially tense. Rebecca sighed. Had it really been such a terrible thing that she had done? When I have children of my own, she thought to herself, I'm going to make sure that they're not glad when I don't come home. I'm going to be a cool parent, like Zoe's mum and dad. I'm going to let my kids do whatever they want.

Rebecca decided to go to bed early. She had a TV in her room and she lay in bed watching game shows until her eyes grew tired. At about half past ten she switched the TV off. The last thing she remembered hearing before she fell asleep was the sound of her mother unloading the dishwasher in the kitchen.

She wasn't sure what it was that woke her up but she felt immediately that something was wrong. It was the same feeling that she used to have when she was little and she would wake up in the middle of the night from a nightmare in which something horrible was advancing towards her step by step and she was totally unable to move. But this time it was not in her dream that something was wrong. It was in the house. She could hear low voices coming from downstairs. There was something about those voices that wasn't right. It didn't sound like her parents talking. She looked at the clock on her bedside table. It was after midnight, very late for her parents to have visitors.

She got out of bed and went to the top of the stairs. A light was on in the lounge. That was where the voices were coming from. She could hear a man speaking now and she was certain it was not her father.

She went downstairs carefully. For some reason she found herself creeping from step to step. She realised that she felt frightened, but frightened of what she could not say.

She had reached the bottom of the stairs now. The door to the lounge was partially open and inside she could see a policewoman and a policeman. They were sitting down on the sofa talking to her mother who was wearing her dressing-gown and pyjamas. She was staring at them as if she could not understand what they were saying.

Rebecca was paralysed with fear. Somehow, they must have found out about the dope that she had smoked. Perhaps Zoe had been caught and she had given them Rebecca's name. She stood there, looking in through the half-open door, her mind racing as it struggled to deal with the situation. Just then her mother turned her head slightly and saw her. She stood up. 'Rebecca,' she said. She sounded desperate. She went over to Rebecca and put her arms around her. Her face was wet with tears.

'What's the matter?' Rebecca asked.

Her mother stood back and looked at her. She shook her head. She was trying to speak but the words wouldn't come out. She took Rebecca's hands, holding on to them as if her life depended on it.

'Mum, please, what's going on?' Rebecca repeated. She was terrified by her mother's behaviour. She wanted to know the worst. Even if she was in trouble. She wanted to know the facts.

Her mother shut her eyes. She was trying to pull herself together. Then she opened them again. All the time the policeman and the policewoman sat incongruously on the sofa, like characters in a play, looking embarrassed by the scene to which they were reluctant witnesses.

'We've had some bad news,' she said at last.

'What do you mean?'

'There's been an accident.'

This was not what Rebecca had expected. She had been waiting for words of reproach. She had been expecting her mother to say, 'Oh Rebecca, how could you have been so stupid?' Instead she had come out with this inexplicable phrase.

'What sort of accident?' Rebecca asked.

'It's Richard,' Carol said. 'He's been in a car crash.'

'Is he hurt?' Rebecca asked. As soon as she said it, she knew it was a stupid question. Of course he was hurt. That was what the police were doing there.

Her mother stared back at her. Tears were running down her face.

'Mum!' Rebecca said. 'Tell me!'

'He's dead,' her mother said. She spoke the words in a whisper but they filled the room.

CHAPTER THREE

The police wanted Carol to go with them to identify the body. She still looked as if she could hardly understand what was happening but she had stopped crying and she was making an effort now to hold herself together.

'Would you like me to stay here with your daughter?' the policewoman asked.

Carol looked at Rebecca who shook her head. She did not want to sit in the house with a uniformed stranger while her mother drove off to look at her father's dead body. The terrible news still hung over her like a gigantic wave frozen at the point of crashing down. Sooner or later that wave would fall with a terrible weight. It would go rushing through the house, washing away every part of the life she had known. But for now it still hung above Rebecca poised in the act of falling. There were no words to explain this. Instead, she looked appealingly at Carol.

'I'll phone Alan and ask him to come over,' Carol said.

Alan was Rebecca's uncle. He was Richard's younger brother and, when Rebecca had been little, Alan had often looked after her while her parents went out for the evening. She liked him. In some ways he was like Richard but in other ways he was very different. His nature was more easy-going.

Carol picked up the telephone receiver and then stood there looking blank. 'I can't remember his number,' she said. 'I just can't...' She looked as if she was about to start crying again.

'It's all right, Mum. I'll get it,' Rebecca said. She crossed the room and opened a drawer in the bureau, found the address book and looked up Alan's number. She felt as if she were a person in a dream, moving about the room and at the same time watching herself doing it.

It took Alan a long time to answer the phone and in the silence the ringing at the end of the line seemed very loud, but at last Alan picked up the phone. 'Sorry to wake you up,' Carol said. 'I'm afraid I've got some bad news. There's been an accident.'

Rebecca could clearly hear him, asking what sort of an accident.

'Would you mind coming over and I'll tell you about it?' Carol said. 'I'm sorry. It's...' But her control slipped just then and she began sobbing. She stood there, holding the telephone against her ear, sobs tearing at her as she struggled to speak. It was horrible to listen to. Rebecca found that she, too, was sobbing.

'What is it? What's happened?' Alan asked. He sounded suddenly frightened.

At last Carol managed to say, 'I can't talk about it over the phone. Please, could you just come over.' Then she put the phone down and gave way to the sobbing.

Rebecca went over and put her arms around her mother.

She didn't want this to be happening. She didn't want to believe it. But she knew that it was real.

'It's not fair,' she said. She knew that was a silly thing to say, that life was never fair. But she didn't see why it had to be her father who was killed. Why not somebody else's. Why hers?

The policeman's radio suddenly burst into life, crackling out a garbled message. 'Excuse me,' he said, standing up. He went out into the hall and spoke quietly into it.

Carol straightened up. 'I'd better go and get ready,' she said, but she was still holding Rebecca's hands in hers, holding them tightly as if she could not bear to let them go. 'Will you be all right while I go with the police?' she asked.

Rebecca sniffed and nodded. 'I'll be fine, Mum.'

'I'll just go and get changed then.'

Carol went upstairs and Rebecca sat down opposite the policewoman. They waited in silence. One thought began hammering at Rebecca's mind: this was her fault. It had happened because of her, because of the way she had behaved towards her father. She had said that she hated him and this was her punishment.

After a few moments Carol came back down. She was dressed now and wearing her coat. 'We'll just wait for my brother-in-law,' she explained to the police. 'He shouldn't be long.'

Time seemed to have slowed down to a near standstill as the four of them sat in the lounge waiting for Alan to arrive. Carol put her arms around Rebecca and hugged her. Apart from that no one moved. They were like figures in a painting. The clock on the mantelpiece laboured painfully from one minute to the next. Over and over again Rebecca found herself thinking that if she had only been a better person her father would not have been killed.

Alan arrived at last. 'What's happened?' he asked, as soon as he got inside.

Carol told him. Alan said nothing for a long time. When he spoke it was almost in a whisper. 'I knew it,' he said. 'As soon as I heard your voice on the phone, I knew it was Richard.'

'I need to go with the police,' Carol said. 'Could you wait here with Rebecca?'

'Of course.'

Carol hugged Rebecca again. 'I've got to go now, darling,' she said. 'You'll be OK with Alan here, won't you?'

'Don't worry about me, Mum, I'll be all right,' Rebecca said.

Carol went out with the police, and Rebecca and Alan were left alone in the house.

'Are you OK?' Alan asked.

Rebecca could not answer him. There were no words to describe how she felt. Her father was dead. She had said that she hated him. Those were the only two things she could think about. She stared back at Alan, struggling to say something in reply.

'It's all right,' he told her. 'It was a stupid question. Of course you're not OK. None of us are. Do you want any tea or coffee or anything?'

Rebecca shook her head. There was only one thing she wanted and that was to go back in time and change things. Suddenly an idea came to her like a candle flame flaring up out of the darkness.

'It might not be him,' she said.

Alan looked confused. 'What?'

'It might not be him,' she repeated. 'We don't know for certain that it is. The police don't know, either. That's why they asked Mum to go and identify the body. It might be somebody else.' The more she said it, the more likely it sounded.

Alan shook his head. 'It's just a formality,' he told her. 'They always do that.'

'How do you know?' The little flame of hope was shrinking back down into the darkness again, but she would not let it go out yet.

'There's no point in getting your hopes up,' he said. 'It's just something they're obliged to do by law.'

'You can't say for certain,' she insisted.

'Rebecca,' he said gently. The way he said it was enough. The candle flame guttered and went out. Of course it was true. There was no point in pretending to herself.

Silence descended on the house again. They sat there, thinking and waiting. A sudden memory came into Rebecca's mind. She was lying on the floor and Richard was lying beside her. She must have been about four years old and he was helping her to make a house from lego bricks. She recalled it all so vividly. She could feel the hard polished surfaces of those bricks, see their bright colours. Where were they now? Up in the loft, probably, or given away. She very much hoped that they had not been given away. The thought of it made her start crying again.

Alan put his arm around her.

'I'm all right,' she told him.

'You think people will be there for ever,' Alan said. 'You never believe this sort of thing can happen to you, or to your family.'

Rebecca nodded. Your parents were just a part of the scenery. You hardly thought of them as separate from you, as people with their own lives. Until something like this happened. Then you realised, when it was too late.

There was a question she badly wanted to ask but she didn't know how to put it. Finally she said, 'Do you believe there is anything after death?' It sounded stupid put like that. 'I mean, do you think people have spirits?' she said.

'I don't know,' Alan said.

'It can't just be the end,' she said. 'It seems so pointless. You're on this earth for so many years and then you're just gone. There must be something else.'

'We just don't know,' Alan said.

'What about the time you saw the pirate?'

'What about it?'

It was a story that Alan had told her when she was about eight years old. She had asked him if he believed in ghosts. It was not the sort of thing she could have asked her mother or father. They would not tell her what they truly believed. They would only say something reassuring to stop her being frightened. She wanted to know what Alan really thought.

He had looked at her for a long time before he had answered. That was one of the things she liked about him. He always treated her questions seriously. 'Not ghosts exactly,' he had replied at last.

This answer had intrigued her. 'What do you mean?' she demanded eagerly.

Alan thought for a long time. Then he said. 'When I was a little boy, a bit younger than you are now, I was asleep in my bedroom one night when I was woken up by the sound of footsteps on the stairs. I thought at first that it was my parents coming to bed but the footsteps didn't carry on past my room like they should have done. Instead they stopped right outside. Then the door opened and somebody stepped in.'

'Who was it?' Rebecca demanded.

'A stranger,' Alan said.

'Were you frightened?'

'Terrified. Too frightened to even open my mouth to call out. I just lay there and watched as this figure crossed the room and stood in front of the dressing-table. I wasn't certain whether it was a man or a woman. It seemed to be a man but he had long hair and his clothes were very strange.'

'What did he do?'

'He opened the drawer of the dressing-table and took something out. Then he turned, crossed the room once more and went out the door.'

'Was that it?'

'Yeah.'

'Did you tell anyone?'

'Of course. The moment he'd gone, it was as if I was released from a spell. I jumped out of bed, rushed into my parents' room and woke them up, jabbering frantically about the stranger.'

'Did they believe you?'

'No. My dad told me I was imagining things but I knew I wasn't. In the end my dad got out of bed and searched the

31

house with me keeping a few paces behind him but there was no one to be found. 'You see', he said, 'it was only a dream.' 'It wasn't a dream,' I said. 'All right then,' he said, patiently, 'you describe this man to me.'

I said the man had long hair, like a woman, and he was wearing strange clothes. 'What sort of clothes?' my dad asked. Then I had an idea. 'He looked like a pirate,' I said. That made my parents laugh. They said it was definitely a dream and they made me go back to bed.'

'And was it a dream?' Rebecca asked, disappointed.

'Wait a minute,' Alan replied. 'I'm not finished yet. I didn't think about the incident again until years later when I was at college, studying for my degree. I was home for the weekend and I was sleeping in my old room. I'd spent the evening having a few drinks with some old school friends. I'd come back late and gone up to my room to get something out of the dressing-table. I glanced in the mirror and suddenly I saw a face I recognised.'

'The pirate?' Rebecca suggested.

'That's right. You see, when I was at college it was the fashion for men to grow their hair long and wear extravagant clothes. The face I saw in the mirror was mine. But it was also the face of the pirate that I had seen when I was eight years old.'

'I don't understand,' Rebecca said.

'That time when I saw the pirate,' Alan explained, 'I was seeing the future. I was seeing myself as I would be ten years later. It was me. I was the pirate.'

'But is it true?' Rebecca asked.

'Absolutely.'

'I don't understand. How can it be possible?'

Alan shrugged. 'Everybody thinks time is a straight line,' he had suggested, 'and that you only move along it in one direction. But what if it isn't?'

It was years ago that he had told her this story but she could remember every detail of it. She thought about his explanation now. If only it were true. If only time were not a straight line and you could go forwards or backwards and change things. If you could do that, then she would go back twenty-four hours and stop herself before she said to her father those three terrible words: 'I hate you.'

'It was true, wasn't it?' Rebecca asked him. It suddenly occurred to her that he might have invented the story to amuse her. 'You didn't just make it up?'

'It was true,' Alan said. 'At least I believed it. But maybe I just imagined the whole thing. Anyway what does it prove?'

'That there's more to life than we know about.'

'Of course there is,' Alan said.

'But what do you think yourself?' Rebecca insisted, 'about life after death I mean.'

'I hope it's true. But that's all I can say.' It wasn't the answer Rebecca had wanted.

It was hours before Carol came back. They had both fallen asleep, where they sat. They were woken by the sound of the key being turned in the lock. Rebecca felt cold and shivery. Her neck was dreadfully stiff from the position in which she had been sitting. She stood up and went out into the hall. Her mother was standing in the doorway. It was no longer night outside and in the morning light her mother's face looked terribly old. Rebecca knew immediately that there had been no mistake.

Carol came inside and shut the door. 'It was him,' she said. She stood in the middle of the room with her coat on. There were still tear stains on her face. She reached out for Rebecca, took her hands and kissed them.

'Poor Richard,' she said. 'One minute he was alive and the next, he was dead.' She shook her head in disbelief. 'But at least he was killed outright. He didn't suffer. That's what they told me. They said he wouldn't have known anything about it. So that's something to be thankful for, don't you think?'

Rebecca nodded half-heartedly. There was nothing to be thankful for as far as she could see. There was only emptiness and pain and the memory of what she had said to her father.

CHAPTER FOUR

'We've got to tell Ben,' Carol said. It was Sunday afternoon. They had finally gone to bed when everyone else was getting up. Rebecca had not been able to get back to sleep and she guessed that Carol had not either, because she was up again a couple of hours later.

Ben was Rebecca's brother. He was twenty-two years old and they had not heard from him for over two years. He had always seemed to Rebecca to be a strange person, distant and preoccupied with his own thoughts. Of course the age gap between them might have been part of the reason for this. But Ben himself was the main reason.

Ben had been a studious boy when he was at school. He worked hard, got good grades and a place at university to study mathematics. He wasn't particularly excited about this. His parents had seemed more pleased than he was. He had settled into university well enough and at the end of his first year he had passed all his exams. But he seemed to become less and less communicative. He never wrote or telephoned and then he no longer wished to come home in the holidays.

Her parents were upset by Ben's rejection, but Rebecca

thought that it was understandable. He was leaving the nest. That seemed obvious to her. She looked forward to the day when her time would come.

Then Ben wrote them a really weird letter. He told them that he had changed his name to Krishna Devi, that he was dropping out of his university course because he could see now that it was pointless – just games with numbers. You had to learn to be single-minded, he said, if you wanted to separate illusion from reality. He wished them well but they must realise that he had a journey which he had to undertake. So this was goodbye for good.

Carol had read the letter out loud to Richard. She was totally baffled by it. 'What's he talking about?' she asked. 'What's this journey?'

'I don't know,' Richard had said, looking grim. He took the letter and read it over himself. 'It sounds to me as if he's having some sort of a nervous breakdown,' he said when he had finished.

'He must have been working too hard,' Carol said. She looked at Rebecca. 'Did he say anything about any of this to you?' she asked.

She shook her head. 'He never talks to me.'

'I can't understand why he wants to change his name.' Carol went on. 'Richard we've got to do something about this.'

The next day instead of going to work, Richard had caught a train to the city where Ben was supposed to be attending university. 'Don't worry,' he had told Carol before he left. 'I'll get him to see sense.'

But he had not got Ben to see sense. He had come back

defeated. Ben, he told Carol, had joined some sort of cult.

'What do you mean "some sort of cult"?' Carol had asked.

'I don't know,' he said, exasperated. 'It's some sort of Eastern thing. It's called Sat Sang.'

'What?'

'Sat Sang. Apparently it means the pure companions.'

'What does it involve?'

Richard sighed. 'As far as I can gather, it involves giving up everything and spending all your time meditating and working for the organisation.'

'But that's such a waste.'

'Of course it is. But it's what he's made up his mind to do. And it's impossible to argue with him.'

'Couldn't he just finish his course at university,' Carol said. 'Then he could do whatever he likes.'

'I suggested that,' Richard said. 'I tried everything I could think of. He wasn't interested. He regards anything other than Sat Sang as a complete waste of time.'

'He must be ill,' Carol said.

But if Ben was ill, it was not with any disease recognised by medicine. Richard and Carol went up to see him several more times but he was adamant that he wasn't going back to university. They grew increasingly frantic. Ben, on the other hand, remained totally calm. His mind was made up. They spoke to his tutor who agreed that Ben was a promising student but pointed out that the university neither wished nor had the power to compel any student to stay on their course. Richard even tried talking to the university doctor but he had no wish to get involved. 'People get religion all the time,' he told them. 'It's not something I can do anything about.'

'This isn't religion,' Richard had objected. 'It's a cult.'

The doctor had shrugged. 'That depends on your point of view,' he said.

In the end things were taken out of their hands. Ben, or Krishna Devi as he now insisted on calling himself, was not prepared to keep arguing with them. When they went to the huge old Victorian house which was the cult's headquarters where Ben was now living, he refused to come down and talk to them. Instead, a polite middle-aged man dressed in orange robes had informed them that Krishna Devi was busy meditating and couldn't be disturbed.

Carol and Richard had been forced to give up. There was nothing else they could do, except possibly kidnap Ben, and this did not seem realistic, though they had discussed it. They had gone back to Beckerton dejected. 'He may grow out of it,' Carol had suggested. She had continued to send him long letters at regular intervals, but she had no idea whether or not he even read them. Certainly, she received no answers. Richard had gone about full of a simmering anger and frustration. Looking back on it now, Rebecca could see that some spark had gone out of him after Ben had joined Sat Sang. He had become more silent, more moody, less ready to see the good in people. Rebecca had never really been close to her brother but she still resented the way he had disappeared so completely and the impact this had had on all their lives.

'Do you think they'll let you talk to him?' Rebecca asked.

'I'll talk to him,' Carol said, 'even if I have to go down there and bang on the door until they let me in.'

She looked so determined when she said this that Rebecca

felt sure Carol would get the news through to him somehow. But would Ben care? That was the question. Or had he lost all memory of the world before Sat Sang?

Carol picked up the telephone and dialled the number of the cult's headquarters. 'Hello,' she said when somebody answered. 'I'd like to speak to Krishna Devi, please. Yes I'm sure he is, but I have to speak to him. I'm sorry if it's against the rules but this is urgent. Yes I know but this is a very serious matter.' She didn't seem to be getting anywhere. 'Who am I speaking to, please?' she demanded. 'And are you the person in charge? Well somebody must be. Yes, I understand that but you should understand how important this is. Very well. This is his mother speaking. I'd rather tell him myself. How do I know that you'll give him the message?' Rebecca wanted to take the telephone from her mother and scream at the person on the other end of the line.

'I want to make one thing clear,' Carol went on. Her voice sounded hard, now. 'If my son does not get this message, I will make trouble for you. Do you understand? Good. I want you to tell him that his father has been killed and to ask him to contact me. Is that clear? Thank you.' She put the telephone down. The tears had come back into her eyes. 'Those people are total zombies,' she said.

'Do you think he will get the message?' Rebecca asked.

'I don't know.' She sighed. 'We'll have to wait and see.'

It was a day dominated by the telephone. Carol had to ring friends to tell them the news. She had to begin making arrangements for the funeral. Rebecca, on the other hand, had nothing to do at all. Everything that she would normally do at a weekend seemed utterly meaningless. She felt numb and at the same time completely exhausted. It was an effort to get up out of the chair. Her body ached as if she was suffering from some sort of illness. She tried turning on the television but she could not concentrate on what people were saying.

In the end she filled up the huge empty spaces of the weekend by doing the sort of jobs that her mother was always asking her to do: tidying up, loading and unloading the dishwasher, making cups of coffee for Carol. Everything that she did required an enormous effort and she seemed always to be moving in slow-motion. But at least she was doing something and that was a way of avoiding thinking about what had happened for a few moments at a time.

For once Carol seemed entirely oblivious to the state of the house. She sat with the telephone glued to her ear and a pen in her hands, making notes about whom she had spoken to and what else needed to be done. After a while the news began to get around. Then the phone started to ring with people calling to say how sorry they were. Each time Carol would answer with the same words, thanking them, explaining that Richard had been killed outright, that he had probably known nothing about it and telling them that she would let them know about the arrangements for the funeral.

In the middle of the afternoon Carol decided to take a shower. 'I'm falling asleep,' she said. 'I won't be long. Would you mind answering the phone if it rings?'

Normally Rebecca would have no hesitation in answering the telephone but now she felt unsure. 'What will I say to people?' she asked.

'Just tell them what's happened, if they don't know,' Carol said. 'If they do, they'll just want to say they're sorry and to know a bit more about what happened.'

'Why do they want to know that?' Rebecca said. It seemed to her that people were just being nosy. Why should she satisfy other people's morbid curiosity?

'It's only natural,' Carol said. 'People want to know what happened. You can't just say he's been killed and that's that.'

Rebecca still didn't feel happy about the idea of answering people's questions but she could see that it was something that had to be faced. 'OK,' she said. 'You go and have your shower.'

As soon as Carol was in the shower, the phone rang. Hesitantly Rebecca picked it up. It was Zoe. 'Hi,' she said. 'How are you?'

Even this straightforward question seemed incredibly difficult to answer. How was she? Devastated was the real answer, but she could not say that to Zoe. 'I'm OK,' she said.

'Are you sure?' said Zoe. 'You sound really strange.'

Only then did Rebecca realise that Zoe didn't know what had happened. Of course. How could she? No one had phoned and told her.

'Rebecca?' said Zoe. 'What's wrong? You've gone all silent.'

At the same time she knew with perfect certainty that her feelings about Zoe had changed. Once upon a time she had thought that Zoe knew everything. That was only twenty-four hours ago but it seemed like another lifetime.

'Beck?'

'I'm here,' Rebecca said. She knew that she sounded

strange. Even to her own ears her voice sounded flat as if all the emotion had been drained out of it.

'What's the matter?' Zoe asked.

Somehow or other Zoe was part of the mistake she had made. If she hadn't been round at Zoe's, she wouldn't have argued with her dad. Well, maybe she would have found something else to argue with him about, but not on that night. Not on the night before he was killed.

'We've had some bad news,' Rebecca said at last. Even as she said it, she remembered that these were the very words her mother had used when she had walked in to the lounge and found her sitting opposite the police, staring at them in disbelief.

'News about what?' Zoe said. 'What do you mean?'

'My dad's been killed,' Rebecca said. It seemed so strange to be saying this, to be admitting it out loud. She felt almost ashamed to hear herself speak the words.

'Oh my God!' Zoe said. 'What happened?'

Rebecca told her the details, just as she had heard Carol tell each caller, how he had been involved in a road accident, how he was killed outright.

'I'm so sorry,' Zoe said.

'So am I,' Rebecca agreed. She meant that she was sorry that it had happened and sorry, too, that she had not been nicer to her father, sorry that she had gone round to Zoe's that night and behaved like a stupid idiot getting drunk and smoking dope and ending up being sick. She was sorry that she could not go back and rub the whole thing out.

'I don't know what to say,' Zoe went on.

'There isn't anything to say,' Rebecca told her. 'I'd better hang up now. There's lots of things to do, you know, arrangements to make, that sort of thing.'

'Right,' Zoe said.

'See you then.'

'See you.' She put the phone down.

CHAPTER FIVE

'What do you want for lunch?' Carol said. It was Monday afternoon, less than forty-eight hours since the news of her dad's death but it already seemed as if a whole lifetime stretched between now and the time before the accident.

'Nothing thanks,' Rebecca said. She was not going to school today. Carol had not even mentioned it. Everything had changed because of her dad's death. The ordinary, everyday world had been left behind. It was as if Rebecca had become a different person overnight. She even saw things differently, more clearly. She realised that she had never really looked at things properly before. But now she noticed the tiniest details. A beam of sunlight was slanting in through the kitchen window and millions of dust motes were dancing about inside it. A few days ago she would not even have stopped to look. Now, she sat there, staring at the tiny specks, which were constantly changing places. That was how she had always imagined atoms to be, tiny dots of matter dancing around in the invisible spaces that were all around us. She felt as if she had to watch this for her father because he would never be able to see such things again.

'You must eat something,' Carol said.

'I'm not hungry.'

'You've got to look after your health, Rebecca. Please eat something.'

When she was at primary school, Rebecca had hated the school dinners, even the smell of them made her feel sick. She could remember that smell now, so very clearly, the smell you get when huge amounts of food are made at a time. It was the smell of people being treated like animals, at least that was how it seemed to her now.

She always brought sandwiches to school but sometimes the smell of school dinners put her off eating even her own sandwiches. Her mother usually made her sandwiches, but some days, when Carol had to go in early to work, her father made them and they were never quite as good. He used all the same ingredients as her mother but for some reason they were never quite as appetising. She would take her father's sandwiches out of her bag, peel back the silver paper, look at them and then wrap them up again. Once or twice he discovered them in the evening, when she had forgotten to throw them away.

'What was wrong with your sandwiches?' he would say.

'Nothing. I just didn't feel hungry.'

She felt ashamed now of not eating those sandwiches. He had done his best.

'I'll have a bowl of cereal,' Rebecca told her mother.

Carol did not look satisfied. 'Is that all?' she asked.

'It's all I want.' Rebecca put the cereal in a bowl and added milk.

'There's someone coming round this afternoon,' Carol said.

'Who?'

'Father Maurice. He's the priest at St Saviour's.'

'St Saviour's?' Rebecca had no idea what her mother was talking about.

'It's the Catholic church. You know, it's past the shopping centre, on the right-hand side.'

Rebecca knew where she meant. But she was puzzled. Her mother had never shown the slightest interest in religion before. 'Why is he coming round?' she asked.

'To talk about the funeral and just to meet us,' Carol said. 'I spoke to him on the telephone and he offered to come over.'

'Is it going to be a religious funeral, then?' Rebecca asked. She had not expected this.

'Yes,' Carol said. 'They generally are, you know.'

'I suppose so. But Dad wasn't religious when he was alive, was he? I mean he never went to church or anything and neither do you.'

'That's true.'

'Well then, doesn't it seem a bit, you know, hypocritical, suddenly going all religious now?'

Carol looked hurt. 'I'm not suddenly going all religious,' she said. 'There's got to be a funeral and I'd rather it was a religious one. Your father was brought up a Catholic, after all. I know he never went to church but Father Maurice says that doesn't matter a bit. He says it's what was in his heart that counts.'

'But he doesn't know what was in Dad's heart,' Rebecca said. 'He never even met him.' She knew that she was in danger of offending her mother but for some reason she felt angry at what the priest had reportedly said. It was as if her father had become public property, just because he was dead.

'Rebecca why are you being like this?' Carol asked.

'Like what?'

'So aggressive.'

'I'm not being aggressive,' Rebecca protested.

'You are.'

'I'm sorry.'

Carol softened. 'What's the matter?' she asked.

'I don't know,' Rebecca said. She could not explain why this business about the priest bothered her so much. She resented the way things had started to happen of their own accord, as if there was a script which had already been written, which was used whenever someone died, and her job and Carol's was to go along with it. She did not see why they had to do exactly what was expected of them.

'I only want to do things properly for him,' Carol said. 'There's nothing wrong with that, is there?'

'No.'

'Well then. You won't be stroppy when Father Maurice comes, will you?'

'Of course I won't.'

Rebecca wondered what it could possibly mean to 'do things properly' for her dad. How could he know anything about it now? Of course, that all depended on what you thought about death, whether you thought it was the end or not. That was something she had not made up her mind about.

When Father Maurice finally did arrive he was not at all like she had expected. She had pictured a stout, middle-aged man with red cheeks and white hair. In fact he was young, thin and rather worried-looking. He was not dressed like a priest. He was wearing a coat that looked too big for him, black cord trousers and a black turtle-neck jumper. He was carrying a briefcase. He took Carol's hand but instead of shaking it, he held it for a moment. 'I'm very sorry about your husband, Mrs Healy,' he said. He sounded to Rebecca as if he was used to saying things like that. He turned to her. 'You must be Rebecca,' he said. He held out his hand, but she could not bring herself to put out her hand to him. She didn't want him pressing her hand. It seemed so phoney.

Father Maurice was not deterred by her reaction. He just nodded. 'This must be a difficult time for you,' he said.

Rebecca said nothing. Of course it was a difficult time for her. It was a stupid thing to say.

Carol said, 'Come in and sit down.' She led the way into the lounge.

Rebecca found herself disliking the way her mother treated the priest with more respect than she would anyone else. In her opinion he was no different to any other man. But she saw Carol looking at her out of the corner of her eye and remembered that she had promised not to be stroppy. She followed them both into the lounge and sat down.

Father Maurice began to explain about the funeral service. 'You'll sit at the front, on the left-hand side,' he said. 'The body will already have been brought to the church by the undertakers. I shall say Mass as usual. Then afterwards, I'll say some prayers beside the coffin. When I've finished the undertakers will pick up the coffin and take it out to the hearse. I will follow them and you will be behind me. We'll go to the cemetery. There will be prayers around the grave and then it will all be over.'

'What's the point, though?' Rebecca asked.

Father Maurice looked puzzled. 'The point of what?' he asked.

'The point of all these prayers. I mean they can't help him now, can they?'

'Rebecca, please...' Carol started to say but Father Maurice interrupted. 'Don't worry,' he told her. 'It's a perfectly reasonable question.' He turned to Rebecca. 'We will be praying for the repose of your father's soul.'

'What does that mean?'

'It means that we pray that he will be with God for all eternity.'

'But why should it make any difference whether we pray or not?' Rebecca said. 'I mean, if there is a God, why should he change his mind just because of something we say? That doesn't really make sense, does it?'

'I don't know,' Father Maurice said.

This surprised Rebecca. 'Well if you don't know, why do it?' she asked.

'It doesn't hurt to try, does it?' he said.

Rebecca could think of no answer to this.

'Sometimes I think the funeral is really there for the people who are left behind,' he went on. 'Other times, well I just hope for the best. Perhaps that isn't what a priest should say, but it's the truth. I know this much though: I hope people will pray for me, when I die.'

'Why did you have to act like that?' Carol asked her, after Father Maurice had left.

'Like what?' Rebecca replied, surprised by the question.

'You were rather hostile to Father Maurice.'

'Was I?' Rebecca asked.

'He's just doing his job, you know,' Carol pointed out, 'which is trying to help people at a difficult time.'

'I know.'

'And it can't hurt to pray for your dad, can it?' Carol went on.

'No I suppose not.'

'Well then?' Carol said. She added, 'I want to do this properly, Becky.'

'I know, Mum,' Rebecca said.

She had not wanted to be difficult. She was surprised herself by how angry Father Maurice's visit had made her feel. Perhaps it was because to him it was just another death. He did not know anything about the circumstances, he had never even met her father. And yet he behaved as if he did.

Afterwards, her mother sat at the table writing. There was nothing for Rebecca to do, except sit and think. She knew that her mother was right. She had not been very nice to the priest. But she couldn't help it. It had just come out. Perhaps she was not a very nice person. She had always assumed that she was. But now she was not so sure. After all, she had been horrible to her father.

'What do you think of this?' Carol said, after a while. She handed a piece of paper to Rebecca.

'What is it?'

'It's a death notice. You put it in the paper to tell people what has happened.'

It read, *Richard James Healey, aged 42, died tragically in a car accident in the early hours of Friday 15th October. A loving husband*

and a good father. He is deeply missed by his wife, Carol, son Benjamin and daughter Rebecca. May he rest in peace.

'Very nice,' Rebecca said.

Carol looked at her uncertainly.

'Honestly,' Rebecca assured her. 'I mean, I'm not really sure what it should sound like, but it seems fine to me.'

'Do you think I've left out anything important?'

'I can't think of anything.'

'Good. I'll take it to the newspaper office, tomorrow.'

Just then the doorbell rang. Carol stood up. 'That's probably Alan,' she said. She went out into the hall and opened the front door.

Rebecca thought about the death notice. It didn't seem very much to say about someone who had spent more than forty years on the earth, but she could not think of anything to add.

Suddenly she became aware that something unexpected was going on. She could hear Carol sobbing out loud. She got up and went to see what was happening. Standing at the front door was a skinny young man. His hair was halfway down his back and he had a long beard. It was Ben. Carol had her arms around him. She turned to Rebecca. 'He's come home,' she sobbed.

'Hello, Ben,' Rebecca started to say but the words did not come out. Instead she found herself weeping. All she could do was shake her head as the tears ran down her face and sobs racked her body. They came from somewhere so deep down inside her that she was completely overwhelmed. Carol reached out and pulled her over. The three of them stood huddled in the doorway, together for the first time in years.

CHAPTER SIX

Ben made it clear right from the start that he wasn't coming home for good. After that first emotional embrace, he stood around looking uncomfortable, as if he suspected that the whole thing was some kind of plot.

'Come into the kitchen and sit down, Ben,' Carol said. 'I'll make a cup of coffee,'

'My name is Krishna Devi,' he said.

'Oh, yes, I forgot.'

Rebecca made up her mind about one thing. She was not going to call him Krishna Devi. He was Ben, her brother, and that was it as far as she was concerned.

'You got the message then?' Carol asked, when they had gone into the kitchen.

'Yes.'

'I wanted to speak to you myself. I didn't think it was right that you should hear the news from someone else, but they wouldn't get you,' she told him.

'I was meditating.'

'So they said.'

Ben had always been a bit weird. At least, that was how it seemed to Rebecca. When he was at school, he was really into science. Other boys his age played football or went to see rock groups. Ben used to read books about the origins of the universe. She could remember him one time, trying to explain to her that the universe was constantly expanding. She had been sent up to his room by their mum to tell him that dinner was ready. She had found him engrossed in a book called *The Big Bang: Fact or Fiction?*

'Dinner's ready,' she had said and turned to leave.

'Do you realise,' he said, looking up from his book, 'that everything in the universe is getting further and further apart all the time?'

'What?'

'Space is continually expanding.'

She stood in the doorway, wondering whether it was worth getting involved in this conversation. She was about nine years old at the time, so Ben must have been fifteen. She knew that he was not really interested in her at all. He was talking to himself. But she wanted her big brother to take notice of her. So she said, 'What do you mean?'

He picked up a balloon. 'OK, this balloon is the universe, right?'

'Right.' She had no idea what he was talking about.

He took a felt-tip pen and drew dots all over the balloon. 'These dots are the galaxies.'

'What are galaxies?'

He sighed irritably. 'Galaxies are clusters of stars.'

She knew better than to ask any more questions.

'Now watch what happens when I blow up the balloon.' He put the balloon in his mouth and blew it up. Then he held it by the neck and looked at her expectantly.

She realised that some kind of response was expected from her. 'It got bigger,' she said.

'Exactly.' He looked pleased with himself. 'And what about the galaxies?'

'The what?'

'Oh for God's sake! The marks I made with the felt-tip pen.'

'Oh. They got bigger too.'

'And further away from each other,' he pointed out triumphantly.

'Ben! Are you coming down for your dinner or not?' Carol called from downstairs.

Ben sighed again and let the air out of the balloon. 'No one else is interested in this stuff except me,' he complained.

Afterwards, when they were sitting at the table, Rebecca had thought hard about what he said, but it didn't make any sense. Finally she had asked him, 'Who's blowing up the balloon?'

He paused with the fork halfway to his mouth and gave her a look that said, 'What kind of life-form is this?' Then he spoke. 'What are you talking about?'

'You said the balloon was the universe.'

'Oh that.' He had already dismissed the whole thing from his mind. No doubt he had moved on to some deeper matter.

'So who's blowing it up?' she asked again.

'It's just an analogy.'

'A what?'

'An analogy. The balloon isn't really the universe. It's just like it in some ways.' He shook his head in despair.

He hadn't really changed since then, not fundamentally

anyway. He was still only interested in what was going on inside his own head. Anyone with any kind of thought for other people, would have realised that insisting on being called Krishna Devi at a time like this was a totally insensitive thing to do. But that was Ben. He might care about the origins of the universe, but he didn't even realise that he might be offending his family.

Carol put a mug of coffee in front of him. 'Well it's good to see you, anyway,' she said.

'Thanks.' He stared down at the coffee as if he was not quite sure what it was. 'Do you mind if I don't drink this?' he asked.

'Of course not,' Carol said. 'What's wrong? Have I put too much milk in it?'

'I don't drink coffee,' he told her.

'Don't you? Tea then?'

'I don't drink tea, unless you've got herbal tea.'

'Herbal tea? Sorry I...'

'It doesn't matter. I'll just have some water.' He stood up.

'I'll get it,' Carol said. She went to the fridge and took out a bottle of mineral water.

'Can I just have tap water?' he asked.

'Are you sure?'

'Certain.'

'OK.'

Carol poured him out a glass of tap water and put it on the table in front of him.

'How did it happen?' he asked.

'He was in a car crash,' Carol said. 'He just lost concentration, I think. Maybe he fell asleep. He was very tired.'

'Was he going fast?'

'Quite fast. It was that stretch of motorway leading to the Blackwall Tunnel.'

'Had he been drinking?'

Carol shook her head. 'Your father never drove when he had anything to drink.'

'Was anyone else involved?'

'No one.'

'So he just drove off the road?'

'Yes.'

'I see.'

They sat around the table in silence while Ben sipped his water. It was hard to know what to say next. 'Are you hungry?' Carol asked at last.

'Not especially.'

'When did you eat last?'

'I'm OK,' Ben said. 'Really.'

Ben was going to be hard work, Rebecca could see that. If he had been slightly weird when he was a teenager, he was twice as bad now. She decided to take the bull by the horns. 'So what's this cult all about then?' she asked him.

He looked irritated. It was the same expression he had worn when she had asked him who was blowing up the balloon. 'It's not a cult,' he told her.

'What is it then?'

'It's just a group of people who help each other.'

'Help each other do what?'

He made a gesture with his hand as if all attempts to say anything further were doomed to failure. 'You wouldn't understand,' he said.

'Why not? I'm not stupid, you know.'

'Rebecca, darling,' Carol said, 'Ben's had a long journey.'

'My name isn't Ben,' he interrupted.

'Yes it is,' Rebecca said. 'It's the name your parents gave you when you were born.' She stood up now, blazing with anger. The legs of the chair grated on the floor as she pushed it behind her. 'Your parents,' she told him, 'and mine, including our dad, who has just been killed.' She spat each word at him.

He sat there with an unfathomable expression on his face. 'I know that,' he said quietly and calmly. 'It's why I'm here. But my name isn't Ben any longer.'

Rebecca suddenly decided she could not put up with any more of this. She turned away from him and went out of the kitchen. She could hear Carol saying something as she left. But she did not want to listen. She went upstairs to her room, closed the door behind her and lay face down on the bed, crying.

After a little while there was a knock on the door. It was Carol. She sat down on the bed beside Rebecca. 'You shouldn't get upset,' she said. 'It doesn't matter what we call him. He's still Ben to us.'

'Why does he have to be so stupid?' Rebecca asked angrily.

'It's difficult for him as well,' Carol said. 'He hasn't seen any of us for years and he's not sure how to act.'

'Whose fault is that?' Rebecca asked with heavy sarcasm.

'Nobody's fault,' Carol said. 'None of this is anyone's fault. OK?' She put her arm round Rebecca.

Rebecca sniffed. 'OK,' she said, a little reluctantly.

'So are you going to come downstairs again?'

'All right.'

Ben was sitting in the same place when she came back down into the kitchen. His glass of water was still more than half full. He acted as if there had been no quarrel at all. 'What's happening about the funeral?' he asked.

'It's at St Saviour's Church on Wednesday,' Carol told him.

'The Catholic church?'

'Yes.'

Ben nodded. Rebecca had expected him to object to this but he seemed unconcerned.

'Have you brought any other clothes with you?' Carol asked.

Ben was wearing grubby blue jeans and a sweater which was unravelling at one of the sleeves. He shook his head. 'No.'

'Were you planning to go to the funeral dressed like that?'

'I hadn't really thought about it.'

Carol bit her lip and said nothing.

'What do you wear normally?' Rebecca asked him. She remembered that her father had said the members of Sat Sang wore orange robes.

'What I'm wearing now.'

'Don't you wear…you know…?' For some reason she felt embarrassed asking him about it, as if it was some detail of his private life that she had no right to enquire about.

'What?' he asked. His face had a look of wide-eyed innocence, as though he had no idea what she could be talking about.

'Orange robes,' she said. It sounded silly when she said it out loud.

Ben shook his head. 'Not me,' he said. 'That's only the monks.'

'You're not a monk then.'

'I told you. I'm just one of a group of people who help each other on the way.'

'On the way where?'

'On the way to enlightenment.'

'Oh right,' she said, sarcastically, 'of course, the way to enlightenment.'

Carol looked anxiously at them both, as if she expected another row to break out, but Rebecca had realised there was no point in shouting at Ben. He could not be reached like that.

He sipped his water and gave her the ghost of a smile. 'You know, you've grown up a lot,' he said.

'Someone had to,' she told him.

The house began to fill up with flowers. Huge bouquets arrived wrapped in cellophane. 'They're lovely,' Carol said, 'but I should have told people to spend the money on donations to charity.' She sighed. 'It would have made more sense. Still, you can't think of everything.'

The flowers lay about in the hallway and in the lounge, waiting for the undertaker to come and take them away.

Rebecca continued to find jobs to fill up her time. She vacuumed the house and washed the kitchen floor.

'You don't have to do that,' Carol told her. 'I'll do it later.'

'It's OK, Mum,' Rebecca said. She felt a certain satisfaction in rubbing the mop fiercely back and forth over the vinyl flooring.

'Well thank you,' Carol said. 'But don't exhaust yourself.'

Ben, on the other hand, spent most of the time up in his bedroom. Rebecca found it annoying that he kept himself so aloof from them, as if he wasn't really part of the family at all, just a visitor. But maybe that was how he saw himself.

He might at least do something around the house, Rebecca said to herself. It seemed to her that he thought of no one but himself. She forgot that she herself had not done much around the house until very recently. The more she thought about the way Ben acted, the more she felt a tide of anger swelling up inside her. She knew that her anger wasn't all to do with Ben, but he was part of it, a part that she could do something about.

She decided to talk to him about it. She knocked on the door of his room. There was no answer. She pushed the door open and peered in. He was sitting cross-legged in the middle of the floor. He had taken off his shoes and socks and they made a little pile in front of him. He was looking at her with a slightly dazed expression, as if he had just woken up from sleep.

'Sorry,' she said. 'I didn't mean to disturb you.' In fact that was exactly what she had meant to do, but she could hardly admit to it.

'It's all right,' Ben said. 'I've just finished.' He got up, sat down on the corner of the bed and began to put on his socks.

'What's it like?' Rebecca asked, sitting down on a chair beside a desk in the corner of the room.

'What's what like?'

'What you were doing. Meditating, or whatever it is?'

'I don't know how to describe it,' Ben said.

'Well what do you think about?'

'You don't think about anything. That's the whole point.'

'So what's it for?'

'I've told you.' He finished tying up his shoelaces and sat up.

'You haven't.'

'It's part of the path to enlightenment.'

'What's enlightenment?'

'I don't know till I get there.'

'God you are such a pain!' Rebecca told him.

'I'm only telling the truth,' Ben said.

'You're not telling me anything.'

'You can't tell people things until they're ready to hear them.' He said this as if this was a truth of incredible profundity.

'I'm ready to hear,' Rebecca said. 'You're just too up yourself to tell me.'

'Up myself?' Ben said with a small smile. 'That's an interesting phrase.'

'It's an accurate description.'

'Why are you so angry with me, Rebecca?' Ben asked her.

'Isn't that obvious.'

Ben shook his head. 'Not to me,' he said. Rebecca opened her mouth to speak but there was so much to say that it was hard to know where to begin. She looked around the room. It was the room that Ben had grown up in and it was just as he had left it when he went to university. Carol had insisted that it be kept that way. She was always convinced that sooner or later he would lose interest in Sat Sang. 'And then he will want to come home,' she would say.

Richard was not so sure. 'When those cults get hold of people, they don't let go of them again easily,' he pointed out.

On the wall above the bed were two posters. One showed the night sky in summer and the other showed it in winter. All the constellations were marked in. She remembered how he had blown up the balloon to explain about the origins of the universe. At least then he had made some attempt to communicate with her.

'Because you don't try,' she told him at last.

'I don't try at what?' he asked.

'At helping. All you do is think about yourself and your stupid enlightenment. You don't care about what anyone else is going through.'

'That's not true,' Ben said. 'I'm here, aren't I?'

Whatever she said, he would continue to reply in that same calm voice. It was infuriating. 'It's all such an act,' she told him.

'What is?'

'All this deep and meaningful stuff.'

'What do you mean?'

'Making out you know all these deep secrets.'

'I don't know anything,' Ben said. 'That's one of the first things they teach you.'

'There you go again,' Rebecca said.

'I'm sorry,' Ben said. 'I obviously can't help annoying you, but I promise you I'm not doing it on purpose.'

Rebecca got up. 'I'm going,' she said.

Ben made a gesture with his hand which seemed to suggest that it was a waste of his time talking to other people, they couldn't possibly understand the important things that were going on in his mind. Rebecca went to her room and lay down on the bed. She had really wanted to talk to Ben, to get through to him. She had wanted to hear what he had to say about their father. She had thought that perhaps he might have said something that would have made her feel better. But she should have known what to expect. Ben was Ben. He was too busy with his own thoughts to have time for anyone else's.

Her eyes began to fill up with tears and she felt a lump in her throat but this time she was not crying for her father. She was crying for herself, because it was all so hard and there was no one for her to talk to. She was locked up inside her head, looking out at the rest of the world like a prisoner looks through the window of his cell.

CHAPTER SEVEN

Rebecca was in the front room in Zoe's house. There were balloons and party streamers hanging from the ceiling. The table next to the wall was piled high with used plastic cups and paper plates smeared with jelly and cake. There were piles of half-eaten sandwiches and a few broken biscuits, some with pink icing and some with brown.

Pop music was playing loudly on the stereo and Rebecca was sitting among a group of little girls in a circle on the floor. They were laughing and giggling and passing an object from one to the other. The object was covered in wrapping paper. It was a game of Pass the Parcel.

It was Zoe's birthday party. She always had the best parties with party food and proper games organised by the adults. Her mother was standing outside the circle watching the little girls. Everyone had big smiles on their faces, both the adults and children – everyone except Rebecca. She was feeling scared, though what exactly she was scared of, she didn't know. She kept thinking that Zoe's mother was looking at her in a peculiar way. But whenever she tried to see if this was true, Zoe's mother was just looking down at the group of girls and smiling.

Suddenly the music stopped. Hannah, who was sitting opposite Rebecca, was left holding the parcel. She sat there for a moment, paralysed by the surprise. Then she began tearing frantically at the wrapping paper. Her face grew more and more excited as she realised that she might be the one to win the present that was hidden beneath the wrapping paper. But before she could get to the end of the layers of paper, the music started again.

'Not quick enough, Hannah,' Zoe's mother called out. 'Pass the parcel!'

Hannah handed the parcel to the girl next to her. Once again it began to travel around the circle. As it got nearer and nearer to her, Rebecca began to get more and more worried. She knew that you ought to be pleased if the parcel stopped with you. But she didn't want it. She was frightened of being the one who opened the parcel, the one that everybody looked at. But she knew, all the same, that this was exactly what was going to happen. The very moment the parcel was passed to her the music stopped.

'Quick, Becky!' voices called out to her. 'Unwrap the parcel!'

She began pulling at the wrapping paper. It was no use hoping that the music would start up again and that she would be allowed to hand the parcel to the next girl. They were all looking at her. She knew now that she had to get to the end of the wrapping paper but there seemed to be so many layers. The parcel kept getting smaller and smaller and then at last the final layer of paper came away. There was nothing inside. The girls all sighed with disappointment. They looked at Rebecca as if it was her fault. Then one by one they got up and began to drift away.

'The party's over,' Zoe's mother said. She was standing looking down at Rebecca who realised that she was the only one left still sitting on the floor. 'Did you bring a coat?'

Rebecca looked at her uncertainly. She had no idea whether she had brought a coat or not. Why was it that she couldn't seem to get anything right?

'Is your father coming to collect you?' Zoe's mother asked. She was looking at Rebecca with concern now, as if she had found her wandering lost in the street.

'I don't know.'

'He should be here by now,' Zoe's mother went on. 'I wonder what's keeping him.'

By now all the other parents had come and collected their children. There was no one left except for Zoe and her mother.

'I want to go to bed now,' Zoe said. She was looking crossly at Rebecca.

'You will soon, darling,' Zoe's mother told her. 'We're just waiting for Rebecca's father. He'll be here soon, won't he Rebecca?' She looked sternly at Rebecca. Rebecca said nothing. She knew that it was all her fault and she wanted to cry but she couldn't, not in front of Zoe and her mother.

'Why hasn't your dad come?' Zoe asked her. 'What's wrong with him?'

Something was wrong with her dad and it was her fault but she could not remember what it was. She wished she had never come to the party. She wished she had not eaten so much party food. She was beginning to feel sick and a little bit dizzy. Things were starting to spin round and round. The harder she tried to remember what was wrong with her dad, the more things went round and round until she couldn't even see the room any more, she could only hear Zoe's voice asking her, 'What's wrong with your dad?' And then she woke up.

She sat up in bed and looked at the clock on the bedside table. It was half past one. She could remember every part of the dream with the utmost clarity. It was horrible. The feeling of physical sickness was still with her. She did not want to go back to sleep again. She decided to go downstairs and get a drink of water.

The light was on in the kitchen. Carol was sitting at the table, writing. She looked up. 'What's the matter?' she asked.

'I just wanted a drink of water.'

'Are you all right?'

'I'm fine.'

Rebecca got herself a glass of water. Then she sat down opposite Carol. 'What are you doing?' she asked.

'Just writing to people,' Carol said. 'It's incredible how many people there are to inform.'

Rebecca sipped her water and thought about the dream. She wasn't sure what it all meant but part of it was clear. Her father would never come and collect her from anywhere any more. 'Mum,' she said.

'Yes.'

'Can I see Dad?'

Carol looked up from her writing.

'His body, you mean?'

'Yes.'

'It wouldn't be a good idea.'

'Why not?'

'He was very badly injured,' Carol said.

At first Rebecca didn't take this in. Of course he was badly injured. He was dead. Then, suddenly she realised what Carol meant.

'They had to cut him out of the car,' Carol said. 'It took them over an hour.'

The full horror of what her mother was describing was too much to think about. 'I don't want to know any more,' Rebecca said.

'OK. That's why I think it wouldn't be a good idea.'

'I know.' She had just wanted to see him for one last time, just to say goodbye, but she knew now that it was impossible.

'We can remember him as he was,' Carol said.

It wasn't enough for Rebecca but she nodded. There was no point in arguing. She couldn't explain to her mother that she wanted some way of making things right, some way of finishing the quarrel she had started with her father. If he were still alive, she could have said sorry. Then he could have forgiven her. But now he was dead, she had to find a way to forgive herself and that was so much harder.

CHAPTER EIGHT

'That looks like wallpaper paste,' Rebecca said. 'Why don't you eat some real food?'

They were all sitting around the table on the morning of the funeral. Ben was eating muesli which he had soaked overnight in water. He did not even have milk with it. This seemed to be what he ate every morning for breakfast. For other meals he ate brown rice and vegetables.

'Is that supposed to be real food?' he asked, pointing to the sugar-coated cereal which she was wolfing down.

'It's delicious,' she told him. 'Try some.' She held up the box.

He gave her a look of mild amusement, as if she were a little child showing him her toys, and carried on eating his muesli slowly and mechanically.

'No wonder you're so thin,' Rebecca told him. She knew she was behaving childishly but Ben was so irritating.

'I'm not thin,' he told her. He spoke calmly as if he were merely correcting a factual inaccuracy.

'Yes you are. You look like a matchstick.'

'Rebecca, don't be silly,' Carol said. 'It's entirely up to Ben what he eats.'

'Thank you,' Ben said.

'Now I want to go through the arrangements for the funeral,' Carol continued. 'I want this to go off properly.'

'It will, Mum,' Rebecca said.

'I want you both ready when the car comes from the undertakers.'

'We will be.'

'Absolutely ready,' Carol went on, disregarding her assurance. 'I don't want any last minute hitches. I want this to go off perfectly, for your father.' Her voice began to crack.

'It's all right,' Ben told her. 'It will be fine.'

Rebecca took her hand.

Carol took a deep breath and regained her composure. She slowly let go of Rebecca's hand, then got up. 'Right,' she said. 'Let's get the breakfast things cleared away.'

Immediately after the washing up had been dealt with, Carol began preparing more food.

'What are you doing?' Rebecca asked her.

'People will want to come to the house after the funeral,' Carol said. 'There's got to be something for them to eat.'

Rebecca hadn't thought of this. 'Do you want me to help you?' she asked.

'Yes please.'

There was something very reassuring about the mechanical process of preparing food. They cut endless slices of cheese and slices of ham, washed and prepared salad, peeled and sliced hard-boiled eggs and opened tins of salmon.

Ben made no attempt to get involved with these preparations. Instead he announced that he was going out for a walk.

'Well don't be too long,' Carol told him. 'Remember what I said about the funeral.'

'I remember,' he said.

How typical of Ben. Rebecca thought, to disappear when there was work to be done. He had always been a bit like that, even when he was a child. Sat Sang seemed only to have made him worse. 'Is he going to the funeral dressed like that?' she asked.

'I suppose so,' Carol said. 'He doesn't seem to have any other clothes.'

'He could at least make an effort.'

Carol sighed. 'I'm just glad he's here,' she said.

They arranged the sandwiches on plates and covered them with plastic film to keep them fresh. They had trouble making room in the refrigerator for all the food.

'We seem to be making enough sandwiches for an army,' Rebecca said. 'Do you think it will all get eaten?'

'I just want to be sure there's enough to go around,' Carol replied firmly.

They finished the sandwiches at last, washed up and cleared away the debris but there was no sign of Ben.

'I hope he's not going to mess us about,' Carol said.

'Why would he do that?'

'Why would he do anything? Ben is a mystery.'

'Does he seem like that to you as well?' Rebecca had assumed that although Ben's behaviour seemed inexplicable to her, it must have made sense, in some way at least, to Carol.

'He's too intelligent for his own good,' Carol said.

'How can you be too intelligent?' Rebecca said.

'You can if you don't have any common sense to go with it. That's my opinion anyway.'

'I'm not like that, though,' Rebecca pointed out.

'No. But Ben takes after your dad.'

'Dad wasn't weird.'

'But he didn't always act in his own best interests,' Carol pointed out.

'How do you mean?'

'He was a bit of a dreamer, too, in his own way,' Carol said.

That didn't sound much like the father that Rebecca knew. She certainly would never have described him as a bit of a dreamer. Before she could say anything, the doorbell rang. Carol went to open it. Rebecca heard her say, 'I don't believe it!' She went out into the hall to see what the fuss was about.

Ben was standing in the doorway, but it was not the Ben who had left the house after breakfast. It was a new, smart Ben. His hair was cut short and his beard was gone. He looked years younger. He was wearing a black suit, white shirt and tie.

'What do you think?' he asked.

'You look wonderful,' Carol said. Then immediately she started to cry.

Ben put his arms around her. It was a slightly awkward gesture. He was obviously not used to this kind of intimacy. But he was certainly trying. Rebecca felt so pleased with him she wanted to kiss him.

'Come on,' he said. 'Let's go inside.' He led Carol into the kitchen. Rebecca closed the front door behind them.

Carol stopped crying after a bit and stood back to get

another look at Ben. 'You look so much like your father,' she said.

It was true that he looked like his father now. Before, with the long hair and beard it was impossible to recognise any likeness. But now it was very obvious.

'What made you do it?' Rebecca asked him.

Ben shrugged. 'Outward appearances don't really matter,' he replied.

The way he said it really irritated Rebecca. He sounded as if he had pondered long and hard on the mysteries of the universe and finally this truth had been revealed to him.

'But they do matter,' Rebecca said. 'That's exactly the point.' He had made a wonderful gesture and then managed to totally ruin it instantly.

'Well I think you look marvellous,' Carol said. 'And now I think it's time we got ready. Come on, Rebecca.'

They went upstairs to get changed. Rebecca took out the black crêpe dress that she planned to wear for the service. She had persuaded Carol to buy it for her the year before when long black dresses had been incredibly trendy but she had only worn it a few times. She never seemed to find the right occasion. Now the occasion had found her.

It was a little bit tighter than she remembered. Perhaps she had put on weight.

Carol was waiting when she came downstairs again. She was wearing a black suit that Rebecca could not remember ever seeing her wear before. The cut was not really in fashion but it looked good on her all the same. She looked at Rebecca and shook her head.

'What's the matter?' Rebecca asked.

'Nothing,' she said. 'Just that I had forgotten how much you've grown until I saw you in that dress.'

'Does it look all right?' Rebecca asked, uncertainly.

'It looks fine. When you wore it before I thought you looked like a child wearing a grown-up dress.'

'And now I don't?'

Carol nodded

'But do I look all right?' Rebecca asked.

'You look lovely.'

'Thanks. So do you, Mum.'

There was nothing to do now except sit down and wait for the car to take them to the funeral.

CHAPTER NINE

There were already quite a few people in the church when they arrived. Among them were a few faces that Rebecca recognised but many that she did not. She had not been prepared for the sight of the coffin. It stood in the centre aisle in front of the altar, resting on wooden supports. It was strange to think that her father's body was lying in this box.

They walked slowly up the aisle to the front pew. Alan was already sitting there along with Rebecca's grandparents. When they sat down Alan leaned over towards Ben. 'Good to see you,' he said, shaking him by the hand.

Ben nodded. He looked slightly dazed at the situation he found himself in. Now that his hair was short and his beard was gone, he reminded Rebecca very much of the boy who spent his time wondering about the origins of the universe.

Father Maurice appeared a few minutes later. He looked quite different in his vestments. 'It's good to see you again,' he told Rebecca. She wondered if he really meant this. Did he really care about the people who came and went in his church? Perhaps he did.

'You must be Ben,' Father Maurice said.

'It's Krishna Devi, actually,' Ben said.

Father Maurice looked confused. 'Well it's good to see you anyway,' he said. He went back into the room behind the altar to get ready for the service.

Rebecca turned to Ben. 'You never give up, do you?' she whispered.

He looked put out. 'I'm just trying to be myself,' he whispered back.

'No you're not,' she said. 'You're trying to be somebody else.'

A bell rang then and two altar boys came out on to the altar. Behind them came Father Maurice himself. Everybody in the church stood up, including Rebecca. The funeral had begun.

The service seemed to last for an incredibly long time. There was a great deal of standing up, sitting down and kneeling. Rebecca had no idea when she was supposed to do each of these. She just did what everybody else did.

After a while Father Maurice moved to one side of the altar and addressed the congregation. 'My dear people,' he said. 'I'd like to begin by thanking you all for coming here today to give thanks for the life of Richard Healy.'

That was an odd way to put it, Rebecca thought – to give thanks for the life of Richard Healy. Still, she supposed that was how a priest might see it. He spoke about what a sad occasion this was, that a young man had been cut down in the prime of his life. To Rebecca's surprise he seemed to know quite a lot about her father. He talked about what Richard had achieved at work and how well he was regarded by his colleagues. 'But above all he will be remembered by those who knew him as a loving husband and a good father,' he said. When Rebecca heard these words she realised that Carol must have told him what to say.

'A poet who lived in Britain a thousand years ago once compared the life of man to that of a bird that flies in through the window of a hall where a feast is taking place,' Father Maurice went on. 'For a moment the bird is surrounded by warmth, conversation, laughter, singing and dancing. Then a few seconds later, it flies out through another window and everything is silent again.'

Rebecca liked that image. In her mind she could picture the bird darting through a room full of drunken warriors.

'But we, who believe in Christ, do not see the world in these terms,' Father Maurice went on. 'For us, this life is simply a preparation for the world to come.'

Rebecca felt much less certain about this sentiment. How could you say that there was a world to come? You would only really know when you were dead. And maybe then you wouldn't know either.

'It is for that reason, that we are not completely downcast today,' Father Maurice went on. 'For we believe that death is not the end of everything and we hope and pray that we shall all of us be reunited in Christ into whose loving arms we commend the soul of our brother Richard. In the name of the Father and the Son and the Holy Ghost.'

Rebecca had hoped that this would be the end. She had begun to feel incredibly tired. She could feel the energy draining away from her and she was struggling to keep from yawning. She wanted to get it all over with, to go home, get into bed and fall into sleep like a stone dropping into water. But the service seemed to be nowhere near over yet. The congregation knelt down again and Father Maurice went back to praying at the altar.

At last the end did come. Father Maurice finished his prayers and the undertaker's men picked up the coffin on their shoulders and carried it out of the church. Father Maurice went behind them and the rest of the congregation followed.

Outside the church the undertaker was busy organising the funeral procession. Richard's coffin was loaded into the hearse. The flowers that had been sent by sympathisers were placed on top. Carol, Ben and Rebecca travelled in the leading car. Alan and Richard's parents were in the next car. After that came a stream of other mourners in their own cars.

On occasions when she had been walking in the street, Rebecca had seen a funeral procession go past. She had sometimes caught a glimpse of the mourners in one of the funeral cars, their clothes black and formal, their faces tear-stained. She had wondered what it must be like to be one of those people, looking out through the window of a funeral car at the ordinary world which was quite unaware of your suffering. Now she was one of those people. Now she knew. It was like picking up some strange fruit that was black and glossy on the outside and biting into the flesh to find the taste was bitter beyond words. But she could not spit it out. She had to chew on that flesh and swallow every bit of the pulp.

By the time they got to the cemetery the day had turned cold. A keen wind blew across the rows and rows of grave-stones. I would hate to be left in a place like this, Rebecca thought. But even as she thought it, she realised that it made no sense.

Her father's grave had been newly dug. The earth was piled up beside it. It looked to Rebecca as though a wound had been opened up in the earth. They stood beside the grave while the coffin was lowered down into the hole. It seemed a terrible thing to be lowering Richard's body into the earth in a wooden box but that was what they were doing while Father Maurice continued to pray. There seemed to Rebecca to be no end to the prayers. 'Eternal rest grant unto him O Lord,' he said. 'May he rest in peace.'

'Amen,' the people murmured.

The undertaker murmured something to Carol. She reached down, took a handful of earth and threw it on the coffin lid. The funeral was over. Rebecca closed her eyes and tried to remember her father as he had been when he had helped her make a house out of lego bricks but this time the memory would not come.

Father Maurice shook hands with Carol, Ben, and then with her. This time she did not withdraw her hand. She did not have the energy. Then one by one the mourners came up and did the same thing. As well as family members there were friends, neighbours, people who had worked with her father. Even her form teacher, Ms Waddell, was there. Each one of them spoke the same words. 'I'm so sorry.'

Rebecca just nodded. She was so tired now that she wanted nothing more than to go home to bed and sleep. Out of the corner of her eye, she was aware of a woman who was standing slightly apart from the other mourners. She was looking in Carol's direction with an expression that Rebecca could not fathom. She waited until almost everyone else had gone. Then she seemed to make up her mind. She walked up to Carol, said something and held out her hand. Carol looked back at her and it seemed to Rebecca that there was something unusually hard about the expression on her face. The woman continued to hold out her hand for a moment longer but Carol made no attempt to take it. Finally the woman turned and walked away.

Rebecca went over to Carol. 'Who was that?' she asked.

'Someone from your dad's work.'

'Why didn't you want to shake her hand?'

'I'm tired of shaking hands,' Carol said.

Rebecca knew how she felt. The funeral had been like an endurance test.

'We'd better be getting back,' Carol told her.

Rebecca nodded. There was nothing more to be done here. They turned their backs on the ranks of the dead and walked together out of the cemetery back into the cold, wintry world of the living.

CHAPTER TEN

It was the day after the funeral that the habit started. It began as just a sniff. Rebecca found that she was sniffing a lot.

'I hope you're not coming down with a cold,' Carol said to her.

'I'm all right,' Rebecca replied.

But it got worse. Every time she sniffed she found herself automatically pulling her upper lip down over her top teeth and slightly flaring her nostrils. She didn't know why she kept doing this. It was just something she had to do. She tried to stop doing it but she couldn't. The need would grow and grow until she had to give in.

She tried to do it only when there was no one watching but it wasn't always possible. Ben must have noticed because he said to her, 'Are you OK?'

She was sitting in the lounge watching television.

'I'm fine,' she told him.

'You should take it easy,' he said but he didn't pursue the matter. Other people's lives were only of marginal interest to Ben.

She carried on watching TV. Ben went up to his room. He

disliked television. He said it was a waste of mental energy. But Rebecca found it therapeutic just to sit there and let the programmes wash over her. It didn't matter whether they were any good or not. It was a release from her own thoughts.

She felt fairly sure that the habit was just a result of her being so tired. It would get better when she had got some rest. That was what she badly needed. The feeling of weariness which had come over her on the day of the funeral seemed to have become a permanent feature of her life. She had gone to bed that night utterly exhausted but had woken up the next morning feeling just as bad. It was as though she had not slept at all.

Over the next few days she did a lot of resting. She sat on the sofa, watching TV or she lay on her bed looking at the pictures in a stack of old magazines she possessed. But it didn't seem to help. She still felt just as tired. The habit was still there, too. It was at its worst in the evenings or whenever she thought of anything stressful, like going back to school for example.

She didn't want to go back to school. In fact she was dreading it. But she knew that she would have to face it very soon.

'I know it's hard, Becky, but you can't allow this to disrupt your education,' Carol told her. 'It's too important.'

There was no point in arguing. Rebecca knew that school had to be faced sooner or later. Finally, it was decided that she would go back to school on the following Monday. Over the weekend she tried not to think about what it would be like but she couldn't help it and whenever she started thinking about school, she found the urge to give in to the sniffing habit was overwhelming.

Monday morning arrived all too soon. She had to get up at seven o'clock to be ready for school but this morning she was awake at six. She lay in bed for an hour trying to go back to sleep. But she couldn't. At seven o'clock Carol put her head around the door. 'Time to get up,' she said.

Rebecca forced herself to get out of bed, get dressed, eat breakfast and pack her school bag. 'Are you going to be OK?' Carol asked her, when she was finally ready to leave.

'I'll be fine,' Rebecca said. But she was far from certain that this was true. She felt very frightened. She wasn't sure what exactly she was frightened of, not the other children, not the teachers, not the school building. And yet somehow it was all of these. It was the outside world that scared her. She didn't want to have to get involved with it again. But she had no choice.

'Bye, Mum,' she said as she opened the door and stepped outside.

'Take care, darling,' Carol replied.

And then she was sucked out of the front door into the everyday world that she had been hiding from since her father's accident. The reality was even worse than she had expected. The journey to school seemed to take for ever. She stood by the bus stop waiting and waiting. Cars, vans and buses drove past at a terrible speed, spewing out exhaust fumes. She could feel the wind whip her face every time a particularly large vehicle went by.

When at last the bus came, she had to squeeze on board with people who pushed and shoved with no regard for anyone else. There was no place to sit. She stood, holding on to a rail to keep from being thrown about the bus.

But the journey was nothing compared to school itself. It was as though she was eleven years old again and arriving there for the first time, only then she had been excited, full of hopes and expectations. This time the thing she wanted to do most of all was to turn around and run.

The first thing that struck her was how incredibly noisy it was. The moment she went in through the gates sounds assaulted her. It was like a zoo. The voices of the other children sounded like the screeching of animals. Boys were rushing about kicking footballs, threatening to mow down anyone who got in their way. Girls were standing around in small groups talking and laughing in voices that pierced her like knives. She wanted to cower against the wall or curl up in a ball but she could not. Instead she took a deep breath and walked into the playground.

The other pupils clearly all knew what had happened to her. She saw them staring. Some of the less tactful ones were even pointing at her as though she were some strange object on display in a museum. She ignored them.

She had not spoken to Zoe since their telephone conversation the day after the accident. She had been at the funeral, or so Carol had told her, but Rebecca had not noticed her. Now she came over to talk to Rebecca.

'Hi Becky,' she said.

'Hi.'

'I'm really sorry about your dad.'

'Yeah. I know.'

They stood there looking at each other. There seemed to be nothing more to say. The silence between them stretched

84

on and on and Rebecca felt as though she were falling into that silence, like falling through space. Then, suddenly the silence was broken by the sound of the electronic pips that signalled the start of the school day. It was an inhuman noise, and it sounded as loud as if it were inside her own head. But at least it removed the need for any further conversation.

Inside the school building the corridors were full of children who pushed past her. They reminded her of rats, rushing about in sewers. She made her way to her form room and stepped inside. It seemed incredibly bright. The strip lights on the ceiling showed up every tiny detail of the room, the scuff marks and graffiti on the walls, the stains on the carpet. People banged their bags down on to tables, scraped the legs of their chairs along the floor and slammed doors. Rebecca stood and waited like a frightened animal.

Ms Waddell came into the room. The noise subsided slightly. She walked straight up to Rebecca. 'It's good to have you back, Rebecca,' she said.

'Thank you, Miss.'

Her words were meant to put Rebecca at her ease, but in fact they had the opposite effect. While Ms Waddell was speaking to her, the rest of the class had been completely silent. Now they were all glancing at her out of the corners of their eyes as Ms Waddell went back to the front of the room and called the register.

Ms Waddell's behaviour set the tone for the rest of the day. Teachers lowered their voices when they spoke to her. Other pupils regarded her watchfully. No doubt they were trying to help but it only made her feel even more isolated.

The school building seemed to her a dreadful place. She

was surprised that she had come here almost every day for years and never noticed this before. Everywhere she looked, things were broken or damaged, paint was peeling off, tiles were cracked, carpet was threadbare. Why did nobody do anything about it? she wondered.

And the teaching seemed to her to be no better. Nothing much was being taught; nothing much was being learnt. Everyone was simply going through the motions. What on earth are they all doing here? she asked herself. But it seemed as if she was the only one asking this question. The others just carried on, unthinkingly, as she herself had done only a matter of days ago.

Zoe tried to talk to her again several times and so did Hannah but Rebecca could not summon up the energy to hold a meaningful conversation with them. She knew that she ought to try but she was using up all her strength just surviving. Her father's death had separated her from all the other pupils at the school, even her closest friends. It was as if they were on a ship which was sailing away into the distance, leaving her alone on a tiny island with nothing but her own thoughts for company.

At the end of the day she couldn't wait to get home. She struggled back through the journey that she had made that morning. When she finally got home she went straight up to her bedroom and threw herself on the bed. All day the nervous habit which she had recently acquired had been driving her crazy. She had struggled to resist it and had only sometimes succeeded. Now she gave in to it completely. She sniffed, she twitched her lip, over and over again. Then she pushed her face into the pillow. That felt better.

'Is that you, Rebecca?' Carol called out.

'Yes, Mum.'

Carol put her head around. 'Did you have a good day?'

'It was OK.'

She came over and sat down on the bed beside Rebecca. 'I know it's hard,' she said. 'Getting back to normal, I mean. But you have to do it.'

'I know.'

'How were your friends?'

Rebecca shrugged. 'OK.' She knew that Carol wanted her to say more, to tell her that everyone had been very nice to her and that she was glad to be back at school. But she could not bring herself to say that.

'Do you think you're going to be able to cope?'

'I expect so.'

Carol kissed Rebecca on the head. 'Well done darling,' she said. 'You're being very brave.'

'Thanks.'

Carol went downstairs again. Rebecca let out a long sigh. Carol thought she understood what it was like, but she had no idea. It was so much harder than she imagined.

In the evening Ben dropped his bombshell. He announced that he would be leaving the next day. He just came out with it as they were sitting around the table eating dinner.

'I'm going tomorrow,' he said, as if he was asking someone to pass the salt.

Carol put her knife and fork down. She looked as if she had been hit in the face. 'Oh no!' she said. 'So soon?'

'I think it's best,' he told her.

'Best for who?' Rebecca asked.

'Best for everyone.'

'Best for you, you mean.'

'Rebecca, don't,' Carol said.

'Well!' Rebecca said indignantly. 'He never thinks about anyone but himself.'

'That's not true,' Ben replied calmly.

'Yes it is.'

'There's no point in arguing about it,' Carol said. She had recovered her composure now. But Rebecca didn't see why Ben should be let off that lightly.

'Go on then!' she said. 'Go back to those stupid friends of yours. After all, they're so much more important than your family.'

'You don't understand,' Ben told her.

'That's all you can say, isn't it? You don't understand. Of course I understand. I understand that you're the worst brother anyone could ever have.' She stood up. She was just about to storm out of the room but Carol's voice stopped her.

'Rebecca, sit down!' she said. She spoke firmly. She had a very determined look on her face. Slowly, Rebecca sat down.

'I don't want any more talk like that,' she said. 'Ben is an adult. He's entitled to come or go as he pleases. Is that clear?'

Rebecca nodded. She sat down.

Carol turned to Ben. 'I'm sorry that you're leaving,' she said. 'We'll miss you.'

'I have to go,' Ben said. 'I promised I wouldn't stay.'

Carol nodded. 'I understand that,' she said. 'Thank you for coming, even if it was only for a short time.'

Ben went the next day. He was there in the morning when

Rebecca left for school but when she came back in the evening, he was gone. She was surprised at how much it hurt. They had got on perfectly well without him for years. Then suddenly he had become one of the family all over again. Now, equally suddenly, he was gone. 'Nothing lasts,' she told herself.

But it wasn't true. Some things did last. The habit was one of them. She had thought it would go away after a few days but it didn't. It had settled down and become her constant companion. It was another thing that separated her from other people. She was the girl whose father had been killed, and the girl with the weird nervous habit.

CHAPTER ELEVEN

It was more than a fortnight since the funeral but Rebecca had still not got over the shock of returning to school. She went through each day like someone in a trance. It was as if she had lost all control over her life. The idea that it was even her life to control now seemed very unlikely. Events just happened. There was nothing she could do about them. She sat in each lesson apparently listening attentively to her teacher. Afterwards she could remember not one word of what had been said.

Zoe and Hannah had given up trying to talk to her. She did not blame them. She knew that she was no fun. But she could not help it. There was nothing about them that interested her. When they spoke, she had to concentrate so hard to listen. Her mind kept drifting off. Their world and her world were two entirely different places. There was no point in trying to build a bridge between them.

The only place that seemed real to her was home. She came back each day from school and shut the door behind her like someone seeking shelter from a raging storm. Carol continued to cope with everything calmly and efficiently. Rebecca couldn't understand how she kept it up. Every evening she sat down at the kitchen table after the dinner things had been cleared away, went through correspondence, made lists of things to do and ticked off tasks that she had already completed.

At least that was how it had been so far. But tonight was different. Carol seemed agitated. She was searching through all the drawers in the bureau which stood in the lounge and it was obvious that she was not having any luck.

'What are you looking for, Mum?' Rebecca asked.

'It's just an insurance policy,' Carol said. She spoke lightly but Rebecca could tell that there was an edge of tension in her voice.

'Is it important?'

Carol straightened up. She sat down on the sofa and for a moment the mask of efficiency slipped and she looked once again like she had on the night she had first heard the news of Richard's death. 'It's very important,' she said. 'It could mean the difference between having enough money and not being able to cope.'

'I'll help you look,' Rebecca said. She had no real idea what she was looking for but she could see that Carol needed support. 'I'll search upstairs,' she said. She went up to her parents' bedroom.

She stood in the middle of the room looking around her. It was hard to know where to begin. There weren't many places that the policy could be hidden. She decided to try the chest of drawers where her father's clothes were kept. She pulled out the drawer and looked at the piles of jumpers, shirts and T-shirts. One by one, she took them out and placed them carefully on the floor. But there was nothing underneath.

'I shall have to do something about Richard's clothes,' Carol had said not long after the funeral. But so far she had done nothing. They lay in neatly folded piles where he had placed them. He had always been a tidy person. Perhaps that was why he found it so hard to put up with untidiness in others. It was one of the things that he used to complain about to Rebecca all the time. He would put his head around her bedroom door to tell her that food was ready and then gasp at the stuff lying all over the floor – dirty clothes, books, magazines, mugs with day-old coffee in them. Then he would start. 'This room is a pigsty. I can't understand how you can sit there in the middle of all that junk and not get up and do something about it.'

Rebecca sighed. It was a speech that she would not hear any more. But there was no relief at this, only a sense of loss. It would not have been so difficult for her to keep things tidy. She wondered now why she could not see that at the time. She closed the drawer and stood up. It seemed to her that everything in this room was stained by grief, the carpet, the furniture, even the paint on the walls. The huge wave of sorrow that had hung over her when she first heard the news of her father's death had washed through the house leaving nothing that was not tainted.

She went over to the wardrobe. His coats and suits were hanging there. His shoes were neatly stacked at the bottom. There was nothing else in the wardrobe at all: no boxes, no briefcase, not even a scrap of paper. She decided she might as well look through the pockets of the coats.

In his overcoat she found a handful of coins, some indigestion tablets and a train ticket. In his mackintosh she found a piece of paper which was folded over several times. She unfolded it and read it, but it was only a list of jobs he had to do; *Phone bank, jacket from cleaners, library books, shampoo, razor blades*, it read. There was something incredibly sad about this list. Rebecca felt tears welling up behind her eyes. She quickly refolded the piece of paper and stuffed it back in the pocket.

This was a pointless task and she knew it. The insurance policy wouldn't be in one of her father's pockets. Still, she decided, she might as well be thorough. Carefully, she felt the pockets of his suits and then a little spasm of hope flared up. There was something quite bulky in the inside pocket of one of the jackets. She put her hand in the pocket and took it out.

It was a letter addressed to Richard. She took it out of the envelope and looked at it. She could tell immediately that it wasn't the insurance policy. For a start it was hand-written. But she began to read it anyway. She had a vague feeling that she shouldn't be doing this. People's letters were supposed to be private. But surely not after they were dead? At least that was what she told herself as she began to read.

Dear Richard,

I am sitting here thinking of last Friday. Your arrival was more welcome to me than any spring could be after a cold winter. The times between your visits are like black holes where nothing has any warmth or any meaning. I have been so confused. As soon as I saw you I wanted to ask you so many things. My mind was full of questions, clamouring to be answered. But tiredness was written across your face. So I said nothing, just opened the door and opened my arms to you.

The things that you said don't make any sense to me. A life of misery is just that – a life of misery. It can be stopped, changed, put right. In the past I have held back too much. But now it's my turn to speak. The very first time I saw you I recognised you. I knew immediately that we had met before we were born, that I had known you in another life. I think that you felt that, too.

I remember the night that you said to me that our friendship was the one thing that kept you going. Well now I, too, am having trouble keeping going. So far I have managed to walk this tightrope and not to over-balance and fall off the edge. But I don't think I can keep on doing this for very much longer. I don't want to fall. I want you beside me, holding my hand. I have no wish to hurt anyone but I want us to have our chance together. Is that too much to ask?

Please, Richard, listen to your heart. You'll know what to do.

All my love,
Maggie xxx

Rebecca stared at the piece of paper which she held in her hand. She could not believe what she had just read. Perhaps she had misunderstood it. She read the letter through again, more slowly this time. But there was no doubt about it. This was a love letter from some woman called Maggie to her father. It was dated about a week before the accident.

She felt shocked, betrayed, disgusted and angry all at the

same time. She immediately found herself remembering the words that the priest had used to describe her father at the funeral, the words that her mother had written on the death notice: *a loving husband and a good father*. So much for that.

Her father had been having an affair. It was such a tacky thing to find out. She wondered how much her mother knew about it. Everything? Or nothing? Should she show her the letter? Would she be devastated if she read it? Or should she just put it back in the pocket of her father's suit and say nothing.

She was standing there going through all this in her mind when she heard her mother's footsteps coming up the stairs. Panic seized her. She couldn't talk about this with her. But neither could she simply stuff the letter back in her father's pocket. She had to think about it. She needed time. She shoved the letter in her own pocket just as her mother came into the room.

'You didn't find anything?' Carol asked.

'There's no insurance policy in here,' Rebecca said, choosing her words carefully. Even as she said this it occurred to her that her father's lies were rubbing off on her. Now she, too, was deceiving her mother. It was a horrible feeling.

'No, I didn't think it would be in here,' Carol said. 'But it must be somewhere. I'll have to phone the company and see if they can help.' Then she looked more closely at Rebecca. 'Are you all right?' she asked.

'I'm fine.'

'You don't look fine. You look awful, actually. You're not coming down with something are you?'

'I'm OK, Mum.'

Carol stepped forward and kissed her lightly on the forehead. 'I shouldn't have got you involved in all this,' she said. 'It'll be all right, honestly. There's no need to worry. It'll turn up somewhere. Your father probably put it in a safe place. You know what he was like?'

Rebecca said nothing. She did not know what her father was like. She used to think that she did. But she had been wrong. He was a different person altogether, a man with secrets. And now he had passed them on to her. It was like learning that you had a hereditary disease, knowledge that you did not wish to have but that you could not avoid no matter how hard you tried.

CHAPTER TWELVE

Carol went back to her lists and correspondence. Rebecca sat in the lounge, pretending to watch television. All the time she could feel the letter burning a hole in her pocket. At ten o'clock she announced that she was going to bed.

'Good idea,' Carol said. 'You could do with an early night.'

As soon as she got upstairs she took the letter out and read it again. Maybe she had been unfair to her father. Maybe it had all been one-sided. But the words of the letter didn't fit that explanation. *I said nothing, just opened the door and opened my arms to you*, the woman had written.

Rebecca could not imagine what this woman, Maggie, must be like but she had obviously been reading too many trashy romances. All that stuff about them knowing each other in another life. It was so incredibly corny. How could her father have fallen for it?

But he obviously had. She wondered if that was who he was seeing on the night of the accident. Her mother had just said that her father was meeting someone after work. Rebecca had assumed it was something to do with his job. But maybe it wasn't. Maybe he was on his way to see Maggie when he was killed. Or on his way back – after she had met him with her wide-open arms.

A wave of anger went through her at the thought of this. Anger at this woman whom she had never even met, but also anger at her father. What a hypocrite he was! She remembered the night she had stayed at Zoe's very late, the way he had shouted at her, calling her selfish, saying she was nothing but trouble. And all the time he was having some sordid little affair with this woman.

She felt herself filling up with frustration and anger. She wondered again whether she ought to show the letter to her mother. Was it better for her to know the truth or to spend the rest of her life believing in a lie? Her mind was full of voices, each one telling her to do a different thing. One voice said that she should keep this secret, because what her mother didn't know couldn't hurt her. But another voice said that her mother had a right to know. And anyway, how could Rebecca keep this to herself? It was too big. Sooner or later it was going to come out.

She could not make up her mind what to do. She could feel a band of pressure tightening across her forehead. She wanted to do something, break something, scream and shout that it wasn't fair. But there was nobody she could talk to. Ben had gone away. She couldn't talk about this to Zoe, or to Alan, or to anyone. It was too much for her to hold on to. She clutched her head, moaning with the struggle.

She could no longer stay just sitting there on the bed. She began to pace up and down. She wished her father could be there so that she could hold the letter up in front of him and say, 'What have you got to say about this, Mr Perfect?'

The skin across her face felt stretched, like a balloon. The nervous habit that had started on the day after the funeral was stronger than ever. She found herself sniffing repeatedly and, at the same time, twitching her nose and her lip until they actually hurt. She felt as if she couldn't breathe. There had to be some kind of release from this.

Slowly and deliberately Rebecca walked over to the wall. She stood there for a moment and then she lunged forwards with her head and hit her forehead against the wall. The pain was shocking and she cried out but in some strange way it also felt good. This was what she needed to do. She paused for a moment and then she did it again as hard as she possibly could. There were tears running down her face now and she was sobbing. The pain in her body and the pain in her mind were the same thing. Again she hit her head against the wall. And again.

Suddenly her mother was in room. She grabbed hold of Rebecca and pulled her away from the wall. 'What are you doing? Rebecca, for God's sake!' she said.

But Rebecca was past speaking now. She stood and sobbed out loud, sucking in the air and letting out raw animal sounds. At first her mother just stared at her, frightened by this appalling transformation. Then she wrapped her arms around Rebecca shushing her as if she were a baby. They stood in the middle of Rebecca's tiny bedroom, tangled up in misery and sorrow, while the pain and the anger continued to pour out of Rebecca with a force that she could not resist.

At last the sobs began to subside. And after a long time, Rebecca began to be conscious of the world around her again and of her mother who was still standing there holding her and talking quietly and calmly.

'I'm sorry,' she said.

'It's all right,' Carol said.

'I couldn't help it,' Rebecca went on because it was true, she couldn't have helped it. The pain and the sobbing came from some place so deep inside her that she could only surrender to them, and at the thought of this she began sobbing again.

'It's all right,' Carol repeated. 'It doesn't matter. Come on. Deep breaths now.'

Rebecca did as she was told, breathing in deeply and letting the air out slowly. Bit by bit she found herself regaining control.

'That's better,' Carol said after a little while. 'Shall we sit down?'

Rebecca nodded and they both sat down on the bed side by side.

'Now then,' Carol said. 'I think you need to tell me what brought this on. But not all at once. Do you understand?'

Rebecca nodded.

'I suppose it was looking through his clothes. I should have thought of that. It didn't occur to me. I thought you were taking it so well, too well I suppose. I should have known. I'm sorry. I've been so caught up with everything I haven't had time...'

'It isn't your fault,' Rebecca managed to say.

'I should have realised,' Carol said.

Rebecca shook her head. 'It wasn't the clothes,' she said.

'Wasn't it? What then?'

Rebecca took the letter out of her pocket and handed it to her mother.

'What's this?' Carol asked.

'I found it in Dad's pocket,' Rebecca told her.

Carol took the letter from her. She looked at the address. Then she looked back at Rebecca. 'It's from Maggie, I suppose,' she said.

Rebecca gasped. 'You knew about her?' she said.

Carol nodded. 'I knew about her,' she said.

CHAPTER THIRTEEN

'But how could you?' Rebecca asked. She was staggered by her mother's admission. In some ways it seemed almost worse than finding out that her father had been having an affair. It meant that her mother was also part of the deception. Everyone knew, apart from me, Rebecca thought.

'How could I what?' Carol asked.

'How could you let him do it?'

Carol gave a bitter little laugh. 'I didn't *let* him,' she said. 'It wasn't as simple as that. I don't know how to explain it to you.'

'Well try,' Rebecca said. 'I'm not an idiot you know, even if everybody seems to think so.'

'Nobody thinks you're an idiot,' Carol said gently. She sighed. 'Your father had lost his way. That's the only way that I can put it. That's something which can happen to anyone. Life is difficult. People make mistakes.'

'That's it?' Rebecca said. 'That's the explanation?'

'Please try not to be so angry,' Carol said. 'It wasn't easy, believe me. Nothing in my life has ever been as hard. But I loved your father. I still love him. And he loved me.'

'How can you say that he loved you when he was having

a…' she couldn't bring herself to say the word, '…a *relationship* with another woman?' Rebecca demanded.

'Because it was true,' Carol insisted. 'People are complicated. Just because he was in love with her doesn't mean he wasn't still in love with me.'

'Of course it does!'

'No, Rebecca. I don't think it does.'

Rebecca wanted to take hold of her mother and shake her. 'So you were prepared to just sit back and let it happen?'

'Of course not. I told your father that he had to choose between her and me and I gave him a certain amount of time to make up his mind.'

'How long?'

'Three months.'

'Three months! You mean all this was going on for three months?'

'Yes.'

'I can't believe I'm hearing this,' Rebecca said.

'You wanted to know.'

'I have a right to know.'

Her mother thought about this. 'Maybe,' she said.

'And did he make up his mind?' Rebecca asked.

'Yes. He was going to finish with her. In fact that was where he went the night he was killed.'

'To see her?'

'Yes. He was on his way there when he was killed.'

Rebecca thought about this. She badly wanted to believe it was true but she suspected that her mother was simply fooling herself. 'It was midnight when the police came to our house,' she said. 'That's a bit late to be going to see someone.'

'The accident happened at about nine o'clock,' Carol reminded her. 'The emergency services had a lot to do before we were informed.'

'So he never even reached her house?' Rebecca asked.

'I don't think so.'

'You don't know.'

'I didn't ask her.'

'You mean you actually know her.' This whole situation seemed to be getting more and more incredible by the moment. She could not imagine her mother coming face to face with this Maggie, but obviously she had.

'We've met. She worked with your dad. You've seen her too, as a matter of fact.'

'What?'

'She was at the funeral.'

Rebecca suddenly remembered the woman who had been standing apart from everybody else, the one who had come over to her mother right at the end and offered her hand. 'The woman whose hand you wouldn't shake?' she said.

'That was her.'

Rebecca tried to picture the woman but it wasn't easy. She had barely glimpsed her and at the time everything had the quality of a bad dream. She had a vague impression of a woman with long brown hair. There didn't seem to be anything very special about her.

'How do you know he was really going to finish with her?' Rebecca asked. 'He could have just been saying that.'

'Your father never lied to me,' her mother said.

'What!' This was the most incredible thing she had heard yet. 'He never lied to you. How can you say that?'

'I knew about Maggie right from the start,' Carol said. 'your father couldn't keep anything secret from me. He was like you in that way.'

'I'm not like him!' Rebecca replied indignantly.

Carol shrugged. 'Well, I won't argue about that,' she said. 'Anyway he came back one evening talking about this new woman at work and I could see right away what was happening. He was so transparent.'

'Then why didn't you stop it?'

'It doesn't work like that, Rebecca. What should I have done? Put my foot down? Told him he couldn't talk to her again? It wouldn't have worked. People only stay together if they want to – if both of them want to. And you can't make someone want to. It has to be their choice.'

'So you let him walk all over you.'

'Nobody walked over anybody.'

Rebecca found this very hard to believe. She felt that her mother was letting her father off the hook much too easily. She was about to say this when the telephone rang.

'Blast the telephone,' Carol said. 'It never stops nowadays.' She went out of the room and down to the kitchen.

Rebecca continued to sit on the bed thinking about what her mother had been saying. Then suddenly she stood up. She went over to the desk in the corner of the room, took Maggie's letter out of the envelope, found a pen and paper and copied out the address which was written at the top of the letter. Then she put the letter back in the envelope. A few moments later Carol returned. She sat back down on the bed again.

'That was Alan,' she said. 'He was just checking to see how we were. He's been very good.'

A sudden thought struck Rebecca. 'Does he know? About that woman, I mean?'

'Of course not,' Carol said. 'Nobody else knew. And that's the way I want to keep it, Rebecca. Do you understand?' She looked earnestly at Rebecca.

'Of course I understand,' Rebecca replied. 'I'm not going to go telling anyone.'

'Good. I know this is hard for you, Rebecca, but I want you to try to think well of your father. You know everybody says and does things that they regret later on.'

'Does that go for you, too?' Rebecca asked.

'Of course,' Carol said. 'Things weren't wonderful between your father and me for a long time. I said things that I regretted. I know he did too. Usually people get the chance to make up for what they've done. They don't always take it, of course. But your father didn't get that chance. He was unlucky. So, does that explain things?'

Rebecca shrugged. Her mother's words about saying things she regretted reminded her of what she had said to her father the night before he was killed. 'Some things,' she said.

'Well it's a start then,' Carol said. She put out her fingers and gently touched Rebecca on the forehead. Rebecca drew back immediately. The touch had hurt. 'You've got a lump on your forehead,' Carol said. 'It'll be black and blue tomorrow.'

'I don't care,' Rebecca said.

'But I do,' Carol insisted. 'I want you to promise me something.'

'What?'

'Promise me you'll never do that again.'

'OK, I promise.'

'I mean it, Rebecca. You must never, ever do such a stupid thing again. ' She put her arms round Rebecca. 'I've lost your father and I've lost Ben. You're all I've got left.' She was crying too now.

'Mum, don't,' Rebecca said. 'I promise I won't do it again, all right?'

Carol sniffed and wiped her eyes. 'OK,' she said. 'I believe you.' She stood up. 'Oh yes, I think maybe I'd better take that letter.' She held out her hand.

Rebecca handed her the letter. 'What are you going to do with it?' she asked.

'Burn it,' Carol said.

'Aren't you going to read it?'

'No,' Carol said. 'I think I've suffered enough without that.'

CHAPTER FOURTEEN

The marks on Rebecca's forehead disappeared quite quickly but the pain and confusion she felt did not fade so easily. She felt now as if she knew nothing. Her parents had deceived her. Who else might have? Maybe nobody ever told the whole truth. These thoughts went round and round in her mind but there was no one she could talk to about them and that was the hardest part. Sometimes she felt as if she must explode, as if she were waiting for a spark.

About two weeks after Rebecca had discovered the letter, her French teacher, Madame Crilly, went sick and a supply teacher was assigned to cover their French lessons. Rebecca had never seen him before and the first impression that she formed of him was not favourable. He was a short man, very overweight, with a red face and going bald on top. He came into the class, told them his name was Mr Caterham and handed out a set of photocopied sheets which their regular teacher had left for them.

'Right,' he said. 'I don't want any talking out of you lot. You know what you've got to do. Just get on with it.'

A girl at the front raised her hand but Mr Caterham shook his head. 'I'm not answering any questions. It's all on the sheets,' he said. 'Just get down to work.'

His attitude made Rebecca feel indignant. It wasn't necessary to talk to them like that. They weren't dogs to be ordered about. Other teachers didn't stride about barking orders like that. And surely it was his job to answer questions. Nevertheless she decided to put it out of her mind and just get on with the work they had been set. It wasn't terribly difficult. They had to write a letter in French to an imaginary pen-pal.

The trouble started with Stephen Bailey. He generally took every chance to be disruptive. He made a coughing noise but was not really coughing at all. He was saying 'Baldy!' in a way that sounded like a cough. People immediately started laughing.

'That's enough of that!' Mr Caterham snapped. 'Just get on with your work, all of you.'

But once something like that had started, it was very hard to make it stop. Now 'Baldy!' was coughed out from several parts of the room. Mr Caterham spun round trying to catch the culprits. This, of course, was exactly what they wanted. People began laughing out loud.

'I said that's enough!' Mr Caterham shouted.

To Rebecca there was nothing even slightly funny about all this. It was boringly predictable. She looked at Zoe who was sitting beside her, grinning all over her face. Zoe waited until Mr Caterham was facing the other way, then she, too, coughed out his nickname. Mr Caterham spun round to face Rebecca. 'What's your name?' he demanded.

'I wasn't doing anything,' Rebecca told him.

'I said, what's your name?' Mr Caterham shouted.

She stared at him for a moment. He had grown even more red in the face and there was a fleck of spittle in the corner of his mouth. She began to feel a huge surge of anger rising inside her. How dare he shout at her like that. He had caused this problem with his attitude. She had just been trying to get on with her work.

'Just leave me alone,' she shouted back at him.

Mr Caterham opened his mouth and shut it again. There was total silence in the classroom now. 'Stand up!' Mr Caterham shouted.

'No!' Rebecca said.

Mr Caterham reached forward to grab Rebecca by the arm. 'Don't you touch me!' she hissed at him.

He stopped just before his fingers closed on her arm. Then he straightened up. 'Get out of this class!' he told her.

She looked straight back at him. 'You get out!' she said.

His eyes widened with amazement. 'Right!' he said. 'We'll see what the head teacher has to say about this.' Then he turned round and marched out of the classroom. As he left a huge cheer went up from the rest of the class.

But Rebecca did not feel like cheering. She was seething. She had wanted to slap him hard across his stupid red face. If he had laid one finger on her, she would have done. She sat there in a pool of cold fury while the buzz of the other pupils filled the room. Suddenly they grew silent again. Mr Caterham had returned, accompanied by the head teacher, Ms Peyton. Mr Caterham walked up to Rebecca. 'This is the girl I told you about,' he said.

Ms Peyton nodded. She spoke in a very quiet voice. 'Rebecca, would you mind coming with me?' she said.

Rebecca just got up out of her chair and followed Ms Peyton.

'Thank you very much, Mr Caterham,' Ms Peyton said, as she left the room.

Ms Peyton led Rebecca down the corridor and into her office. 'Now then, Rebecca,' she said when they were sitting down. 'I understand you got involved in a confrontation with Mr Caterham.'

'I wasn't do anything,' Rebecca insisted. 'He just started picking on me.' When she had stood up to Mr Caterham, it had been easy to keep calm. Fury had kept her other emotions under control. But now, faced with Ms Peyton's gentle tone, Rebecca felt her eyes filling up with tears and she struggled to get her words out.

'All right, Rebecca,' Ms Peyton said. 'I'm not accusing you of anything. I'm just saying that you got involved in a confrontation. Now would you like to tell me your side of the story?'

'People were messing about,' Rebecca said, 'but I wasn't one of them and then he started shouting at me and it wasn't fair…' She could not say any more because of the sobs that kept rising up inside her.

'All right, Rebecca,' Ms Peyton said. 'I believe you. I expect Mr Caterham just made a mistake. That sort of thing can happen when a teacher is not familiar with the class. Unfortunately nobody has told him about your particular circumstances. They certainly should have. That was our fault. But I can't have pupils talking to teachers in the way that you spoke to Mr Caterham. I'm sure you can see that.'

'Yes, Miss.'

'Good.' She gave Rebecca her big smile which she usually reserved for making announcements at assembly about pupils who had done exceptionally well. 'I think the best thing is for you to just sit here and calm down for a while. Don't you agree?'

'Yes, Miss.'

'Actually Rebecca,' Ms Peyton went on. 'I was wondering whether you'd had the chance to talk to anybody about what you've been through recently?'

Rebecca looked at her in surprise. 'I don't know what you mean, Miss,' she said.

'Anyone other than your family and friends, I mean. A professional person.'

Rebecca shook her head. She was still not sure what Ms Peyton was getting at.

'We're fortunate to have attached to the school, a very good counsellor. I know she'd be happy to talk to you, if you'd like that.'

So that was what she meant. Rebecca had not expected this. She looked blankly back at Ms Peyton. The thought of telling someone everything that had happened was immensely attractive in one way. It was what she had wanted ever since her father's death. But at the same time she knew that it was impossible. Her problems were far too private.

'Of course there's no compulsion,' Ms Peyton went on. 'It's entirely up to you. But people do find it helpful. Everything would be in complete confidence, naturally. No one else would be involved. You don't have to make up your mind right now. Think about it. Let me know.'

'Yes, Miss.'

Rebecca did not rejoin her class until lunchtime. When she did a group of girls gathered around, eyeing her with a kind of wary approval. Zoe, who was among them, asked what Ms Peyton had said.

'Nothing,' Rebecca told her.

'You weren't in trouble then?'

Rebecca shook her head. Compared to what had happened to her in the last few weeks an interview with the head teacher could hardly be described as trouble. When they saw that Rebecca would not be any more forthcoming, the girls eventually drifted away, even Zoe.

Rebecca returned to thinking about what Ms Peyton had said. Talking to anyone about her experience meant telling them about the letter. She was not sure that was something she was prepared to do. It was too shameful. For her mother it might be possible just to burn the letter and forget about it, but not for Rebecca. She brooded over the letter, and in her mind she kept seeing the image of Maggie coming up to her mother at the end of the funeral, offering her hand and her mother turning away, her face a mask of pain and weariness.

A few days later when Rebecca was on her way to the school dining room, Ms Peyton came up to her again. 'How are you today, Rebecca?' she asked.

'Fine thanks.'

'I wondered if you'd thought any more about our conversation,' Ms Peyton went on.

Rebecca shook her head. 'I don't know,' she said.

'Well why don't you just come along and meet Ms Vine, our counsellor. Then you can see what you think?'

'OK, Miss.' There didn't seem much else that Rebecca could say.

That night, after they had eaten, Rebecca said to Carol, 'Ms Peyton asked if I wanted to see a counsellor.'

Her mother, who had been loading the dishwasher, stopped what she was doing and stood up. 'And what did you say?' she asked. She looked anxious.

'I said I'd think about it.'

'Well if you think it would help, perhaps it would be a good idea.' She spoke without much conviction.

'I'm not sure,' Rebecca said.

'What sort of thing would you talk about?' Carol asked. There was an edge of tension in her voice. It seemed to Rebecca that her mother was worried about what she might say.

'I don't know. Problems, I suppose,' Rebecca said.

'Have there been any problems? I mean at school.'

'Not really.' It was a lie but she did not want her mother to know about the incident with Mr Caterham.

'Well it's up to you,' Carol said. 'You don't have to do anything you don't want to.'

'I know that, Mum.'

'And if you want to talk to me about anything, I'm always here.'

'I know that, too.'

But it was not as simple as that. Lying in bed that night Rebecca went over what her mother had told her about her father's last journey, how he had been going to tell Maggie that it was all over between them. There was no proof of this. It was something that had to be taken on trust, but Rebecca thought that it could be true. She felt sure that her mother believed it. What a pity then that he had never reached the house, that the message had not been delivered.

Ms Peyton had arranged for Rebecca to meet the counsellor after lunch on Friday. All that morning Rebecca found herself dreading the encounter. The nervous habit which she had developed after the funeral seemed to tighten its grip on her. She found herself sitting in class, sniffing repeatedly and she noticed some of the other pupils staring at her.

The thing that was really beginning to bug her was that Maggie had never known the truth. She would always believe that she and Rebecca's father were going to have their chance together, as she put it in that tacky little letter. She didn't know that her time was up because Rebecca's father didn't get the chance to tell her. The more Rebecca thought about this, the more she wished that her father had finished the job he set off to do that night.

After lunch, when everyone else went back to class, Rebecca was supposed to go and talk to the counsellor and she had made up her mind that this was what she was going to do. After all it couldn't hurt to just go along and meet her. But as Rebecca drew nearer to the office at the front of the school where the meeting was scheduled, she felt more and more reluctant to go. She began walking more and more slowly. Finally she paused outside the office door. She put out her hand to knock but stopped.

An idea had taken shape in her imagination that was far more attractive than talking to the school counsellor. She saw herself walking up to the front door of a house, ringing the bell and waiting. She saw a woman answering, the woman who had come up to her mother after the funeral. And then she would introduce herself. She imagined the look of shock spreading over the woman's face as she realised whom she was talking to. And then the woman would burst into tears when Rebecca said what she had come to say. Finally, Rebecca would turn and walk away leaving the woman weeping on her own doorstep. It was a very satisfying picture.

As Rebecca thought about this, it seemed not just possible but necessary. Someone had to do it. Her father had been prevented by a piece of bad luck. Her mother would never do it. As far as she was concerned the episode was closed. Rebecca was the only one left.

She turned and walked away from the counsellor's office but not back in the direction of her class. Instead she went out through the front door into the street. She was going to see Maggie. At the time that she did it, Rebecca had not really known why she had decided to copy out the address at the top of Maggie's letter. She had just had a strong sense that the whole thing was not over yet. Now she knew why. This was what she had been meaning to do all along.

Maggie lived in North London. Rebecca had already looked up the address in the street map. It was not far from a tube station. So there would be no difficulty getting there. She had butterflies in her stomach at the thought of what she was going to do and her nervous habit kept demanding her attention, insisting that she give in to it. But she was not going to be put off now. She had a mission and she was not going to fail.

It made her so angry when she thought about what Maggie

had written in the letter. She had made it sound so marvellous and poetic when all she was doing was breaking into someone else's family, trying to steal part of their life, using their happiness to cheer up her own miserable little life. That was how she imagined her – miserable, pathetic – a lonely middle-aged woman who had failed to find a proper partner for herself. So instead she had to go around trying to steal someone else's.

As she waited at the tube station, Rebecca went over and over what she was going to say to Maggie. It was a speech laced with irony. She would announce who she was right away. 'I don't suppose you expected a visit from me,' she would add. 'That wasn't part of your calculations, was it?' She felt immense satisfaction at the thought of how Maggie would react to this. And that was only the beginning.

Rebecca wondered whether her father knew what she was doing. She hoped he did. She still didn't know what she thought about this. Maybe there was some sort of afterlife. Maybe there wasn't. But even if there was nothing, even if her father was wiped out completely, she was carrying on for him. In a way she was her father's afterlife and she was going to try and make sure it turned out right this time. She felt no pity for Maggie. The woman was a kind of emotional parasite. She deserved everything she got.

In forty minutes Rebecca had reached her destination. She got off the train and the escalator brought her back to the surface again, blinking at the bright daylight. As she set off for Maggie's house, she began to feel her courage draining away from her. Now the whole thing began to seem like a ridiculous idea. She was just a child meddling in an adult world. Why had she not just gone to see the counsellor as she was supposed to? But still her legs continued to lead her in the direction of Maggie's house.

What if her mother had got it all wrong? she asked herself. What if her father had actually been to see Maggie on that night? Perhaps he had been lying all the time. She had reached Maggie's road now, a long line of Victorian houses, a little shabbier than she had expected. Many of them had been turned into separate apartments. Most of them were in need of painting. She looked at the numbers on the doors and began to count the houses that still remained before she reached her destination. Only twenty left. Nineteen. Eighteen. She was walking much more slowly and she wished that she were not here at all. It was a stupid idea. Her father was dead. Nothing that she said to this woman could change that.

Now she was right outside Maggie's apartment but she kept right on walking past. She just could not go up to that door and ring the bell. She carried on walking for about a minute and then she stopped. This was ridiculous! She had skipped her appointment with the counsellor, bunked off school, come all this way and now she couldn't even bring herself to go through with it. Well that wasn't good enough. She was going to do it.

She turned and retraced her steps. Suddenly she realised that Maggie would probably not even be at home. It was a weekday, after all. She was bound to be at work. How stupid she had been! For some reason this hadn't even occurred to her before. Well at least that would let her off the hook. She could ring the bell, wait, then turn and go back to the station.

It would all be over. She would have tried her best and just been unlucky.

She was level with Maggie's door again. This was it. But still she couldn't quite pluck up the courage to go through with it. What if she was in? Then Rebecca would have to say what she had come here to say, except that her little speech sounded rather feeble now, when she ran through it again in her mind.

She was sniffing and twitching. She knew that. But she couldn't help herself. She was completely powerless either to go up to the door and ring the bell or turn and walk away. She was caught in a trap that she had made for herself.

'Come on, Rebecca,' she told herself. 'You've got to do better than this. You've got to do it. You know you have.'

Suddenly the front door opened and a woman came out. It was her. Rebecca stood frozen to the spot as Maggie walked down the path towards her. Then she stopped and stood facing her. There was a moment of silence that seemed to stretch on for ever and ever. Then Maggie spoke. 'It's Rebecca, isn't it?' she said. 'I've been watching you for some time. I think you'd better come inside, don't you?'

CHAPTER FIFTEEN

Maggie did not look much like the person Rebecca thought she had remembered. She had caught only the briefest of glimpses of her at the funeral and had built up in her mind a picture of someone much more glamorous than her mother and somehow subtly but unmistakably evil – a bit like the wicked queen in a fairy story. This woman was nothing like that. She was about the same age as Rebecca's mother. Her hair was cut short in a style that suited her, and dyed a reddish colour. The clothes she was wearing were anything but glamorous. She had on a sweat shirt and jeans, but all the same, there was something about her that suggested confidence in her appearance. Rebecca followed her meekly inside.

The interior of the house had been decorated with the same sense of confidence in the owner's taste. It was an old house but the two front rooms had been knocked through to create one large living space with a pine staircase against one wall. The floorboards had been stripped and varnished and covered with rugs in ethnic designs. The lighting was subdued. The walls were painted off-white and hung with pictures.

'Please sit down,' Maggie said.

Rebecca sat down on a big comfortable sofa facing the street. It occurred to her that this was probably exactly where Maggie herself had been sitting only a few moments earlier, watching her as she stood outside trying to pluck up the courage to enter. She found herself blushing at the thought.

'Would you like a cup of tea?' Maggie asked.

'OK,' Rebecca said. Now that she was actually inside this woman's house, she found it hard even to speak. A few moments ago she had still been in control. Now she felt as if that control had been completely taken away from her. The things that she had thought about saying on the way here were forgotten.

Maggie disappeared into the back of the house leaving Rebecca to sit and look about the room. The furniture was a mixture of modern and antique but everything had been chosen carefully to work together. Everywhere you looked there were interesting objects but somehow the room itself remained uncluttered. Everything was in its place. 'But it's not lived-in,' Rebecca told herself defiantly.

She could not help wondering what it was about this woman that had made her father prefer her to her mother, even if only for a short time. Was it this elegance, which she found so intimidating? Or was it because Maggie's house was so very unlike their own? There was no chaos here, no evidence of other people's lives, and certainly no children.

She got up and went to look more closely at what seemed to be a piece of modern art. It turned out to be a collection of shells mounted in a display case. Each one of the shells was different but the insides of them all were lined with silvery mother-of-pearl.

'Do you like them?' Maggie asked, coming back into the room with a tray on which were placed a teapot, two china cups and saucers, a china milk jug and a silver sugar bowl.

'They're very nice,' Rebecca said carefully.

Maggie put the tray down on a low glass table beside the sofa. Then she came over and stood beside Rebecca. 'I collected them from a beach in Cornwall,' she said. 'It was littered with them. Afterwards I decided I just had to frame them.'

Rebecca wanted to say, 'So it's not just other women's husbands that you collect?' but she did not feel brave enough. Instead she sat down on the sofa again and waited for Maggie to pour the tea.

'Milk and sugar?' Maggie asked.

'Just milk please.'

The cup was so delicate that Rebecca felt it might break in her hand. She sipped her tea carefully.

'I'm so glad you came,' Maggie said.

This was not at all how Rebecca had expected her to feel. She was annoyed by the woman's composure. 'How did you recognise me?' she asked.

'I saw you at the funeral.'

'Oh yes.'

'I think it was very brave of you to come here.'

'Do you?'

'Yes I do. After all, you must hate me,' Maggie went on. 'And I don't blame you for that.'

Every word she said irritated Rebecca even further. The

calm, polished manner that she used seemed designed to keep Rebecca in her place, to remind her that she was only a child.

'I don't hate you at all,' Rebecca said. She hadn't meant to say this but she was not going to let Maggie have things all her own way. 'I don't really care about you one way or the other.'

'But you came to see me,' Maggie pointed out.

'I was curious.'

'Well that's a start,' Maggie said. It seemed a funny thing to say and Rebecca could think of nothing to add in reply. She sipped her tea instead.

'You know I never wanted to hurt you, or your mother. And that's the truth.'

Rebecca raised one eyebrow. It was something she had learnt to do when she was little. She had practised it in front of a mirror. She knew the effect it had. It made her look as if she could see perfectly well that the person she was listening to was lying.

'You don't believe me? Well it's true, anyway,' Maggie went on. 'I just couldn't help loving your father, that's all.'

'You didn't have to do something about it, though,' Rebecca said.

'You might think differently about that when you're older,' Maggie replied.

'No, I won't.'

Maggie smiled patiently at her. 'We'll just have to wait and see, then, won't we?' She spoke as if Rebecca was about four years old. She lifted the teapot. 'Would you like some more tea?'

'I haven't finished this cup yet.'

Maggie put the teapot down again. 'Richard talked such a lot about you,' she said.

That really hurt. To hear this woman using her father's name as if she had a right to do so, and acting as if she knew all about Rebecca's life, stung her into remembering what she had come to do. She opened her mouth to say that her father was going to finish their relationship on the night that he was killed, but what Maggie said next stopped her in her tracks.

'In a way I envy your mother,' she said. 'Does that sound a terrible thing to say?'

It did sound a terrible thing to say. Such a terrible thing that Rebecca could not speak. She found herself growing dizzy. She put her hands up to her head for a moment to steady herself but Maggie did not seem to notice. 'She has you,' she went on, speaking in the same calm, quiet voice. 'For me, there's nothing left. Do you understand that?'

Rebecca stared back at her. Suddenly, to her horror, Maggie started to cry. Not loudly but quietly, sniffling to herself.

Rebecca didn't know what to do. So many conflicting emotions filled her. She felt disgusted with this woman for behaving like this. She wanted to shout at her, 'For God's sake who do you think you are?' but what Maggie had said prevented her because she suddenly saw that it was true. For her there was nothing left. Rebecca's father was gone and so was the life she had tried to build with him.

'I'm sorry,' Maggie said, producing a small handkerchief from somewhere and blowing her nose. 'I shouldn't have said that. It was just you coming here today.'

That was why she had been so pleased to see her, Rebecca realised. It was a tiny bit of her old life returning. She had imagined that Maggie would be appalled to see her but she had been wrong. She had been delighted. Well Rebecca wasn't going to give her the satisfaction of prolonging the visit any longer. 'I've got to go now,' she said, suddenly standing up.

'Oh don't go yet!' Maggie said. There was a new, slightly pathetic note in her voice. She sounded as if she were pleading.

But Rebecca's mind was made up. There was no reason for her to be here now. She wanted to get out of the house as quickly as she could. 'I have to go,' she said. She no longer felt intimidated by this elegant room with its expensive furnishings. The balance had shifted. Now it seemed to her to be an empty place, like a museum, and Maggie was its curator. For a while she had managed to contain a part of Rebecca's father's life within these walls, but it was never more than a fragment out of which she had sought to build a reality, like someone who tries to imagine the everyday life of a society from a few pieces of broken pottery that they have unearthed.

Maggie stood up. She took Rebecca's hand. 'Your father was the most wonderful man I ever met,' she said. 'I really loved him. I want you to know that.'

Rebecca nodded. Gently, she detached her arm from Maggie's grip. 'Thanks for the tea,' she said. She went out into the hall.

Maggie followed her to the door. 'Come and see me again,' she said, 'whenever you like.'

Rebecca made no reply. She opened the door and stepped outside. It felt like a huge release. She took a deep breath. 'Goodbye then,' she said, without turning round. She walked down the path and out of the gate.

Only when she was halfway to the tube station did it occur to her that she had not done what she had gone there to do: she had not told Maggie that Richard had intended to finish his relationship with her. But it did not seem to matter. She no longer cared what Maggie thought.

She felt for the first time that she understood her mother's attitude to the affair. She had wondered how her mother had put up with it, why she had not screamed and shouted and thrown her father out of the house. Now she thought she could guess. Her mother had seen the whole picture, not just the part of her father's life that Maggie knew. She had known what Rebecca's father was really like, what was good about him and what was imperfect. She hadn't worshipped him. But she had loved him, just as Rebecca had done. Theirs was a real life together, the life of a family who had struggled to live with each other, sometimes quarrelling but ultimately forgiving each other and that was a life worth living. Her mother had not tried to keep him against his will because in the end it was his choice and for the first time Rebecca felt sure which choice he had made. On the night he was killed her father had planned to tell Maggie that it was all over between them. That was what her mother had told her and that was what she believed. No one had known her father better than her mother.

CHAPTER SIXTEEN

On Saturday Rebecca called round to see Zoe. At first Zoe looked surprised to see her at the door but she tried to act as she had always done. 'Come on up,' she said.

It was the first time she had been to Zoe's house since the night her father had called to collect her and she could not help thinking about this as she followed Zoe up the stairs to the top of the house. She remembered listening to his voice on the answerphone and wishing her parents could be more like Zoe's. All that seemed to have taken place in another life-time when she was somebody else altogether.

They sat down in Zoe's room just as they had been accustomed to doing but the atmosphere was slightly tense between them. Rebecca looked around the room taking in every detail: the bottles with their multi-coloured coatings of wax where candles had dripped down on them, the posters on the walls that seemed to look different depending on which angle you viewed them from, the beautiful Indian bedspread that Zoe's mother had bought her. Rebecca had envied Zoe all of this once. Now it seemed to her to be just another room and Zoe to be just another schoolgirl. She wondered what all the fuss had been about.

'How are you?' Zoe asked.

Rebecca shrugged. 'I'm all right,' she said.

'I didn't know whether to phone you, or come round or what,' Zoe said apologetically. 'I thought maybe you just wanted to be left alone.'

'I did for a while.'

'It must have been a terrible time. I mean, I know that sounds stupid...' Zoe said.

She was trying to say the right thing, Rebecca could see that. But really there was no right thing to say. 'It's all right,' she told her. 'It doesn't sound stupid. Yeah, it's been terrible but, you know, there's nothing anyone can do about it so...' She shrugged.

Zoe nodded. 'I don't know how I would have dealt with it,' she said, 'if it had been me, I mean.'

'You just do,' Rebecca told her.

'Well, you know, if you want to talk about it or anything.'

Rebecca shook her head. 'There isn't very much to talk about,' she said. That wasn't quite true. Really, there was far too much to talk about. But it was as close as she could get to explaining it to Zoe.

'Or if there's anything I can do,' Zoe said.

It seemed to Rebecca that there was nothing in the world that Zoe could possibly do which would make things even one bit better. She almost said as much but then it occurred to her that perhaps it was not true. She had come here, after all, to see the girl who had been her best friend. Deep down, she knew that she wanted that relationship back. 'Let's listen to some music,' she suggested.

Zoe looked pleased with this suggestion. This was familiar

territory. 'Got any requests?' she asked.

'You choose,' Rebecca told her.

Zoe took a CD and put it in the player. A moment later a drum beat began throbbing and music burst out of the speakers. Rebecca felt a thrill of recognition. It was one of her favourites. She had not realised how much she had missed listening to music.

It was easier now between them. The music filled up the gaps in their conversation. And after a while, Rebecca felt herself beginning to relax. 'So what's been happening?' she asked.

Zoe gave an odd grin. She managed to look both embarrassed and pleased with herself at the same time. 'Guess what?' she said. 'I've got a boyfriend.' She tried to sound as casual as possible about it, but she was obviously delighted to have the opportunity to talk about it.

'Congratulations,' Rebecca said. 'What's his name?'

'Jamie.'

Rebecca considered this. It wasn't a bad name. 'Jamie what?' she asked.

'Jamie Lewis,' Zoe said. The reason for her embarrassment became obvious.

'Not Jamie Lewis who plays the trombone?' Rebecca asked.

'That's him.'

Jamie Lewis was hardly the world's greatest catch. He was a year older than Zoe and he was tall, both of which were in his favour, but he was a bit of a drip. For a start he had no sense of fashion. His clothes always looked too big for him and his hair looked like his mother cut it with a pudding basin and a pair of scissors. He was in the school orchestra and was always to be seen lugging his trombone around in its case, coming and going from rehearsals. There was definitely something faintly ridiculous about him. Rebecca would never have thought of him as a possible boyfriend for anyone, least of all Zoe.

'I think he's got potential,' Zoe said.

Rebecca thought about this. Maybe she was right. After all someone like Zoe wouldn't want a boyfriend with a strong personality. She would want someone who would fall in with all her plans. 'How did it start?' she asked.

'At a party last week,' Zoe said. 'It was somebody's birthday. I can't remember whose, but there were a lot of musical types there. He just came over to me and, well you know...'

Rebecca did not really know. This side of things still seemed rather a mystery to her. She strongly suspected it would remain a mystery for some time to come. She sniffed, twitched her nose, then asked, 'Is he nice?'

'He's OK,' Zoe said. 'He uses this really weird aftershave, or maybe it's his deodorant, I'm not sure.'

'In what way weird?' Rebecca asked.

'It smells a bit like Christmas cake,' Zoe said.

'Christmas cake!' Rebecca said.

'I swear it's true,' Zoe said. She started to giggle. 'My mum always buys this Christmas cake every year and that's exactly what he smells like.'

Rebecca found that she was giggling too. 'That is weird,' she agreed.

'But quite nice,' Zoe said. 'I like Christmas cake.' She giggled again.

'So that's the main news, is it?' Rebecca said. 'You're going out with Jamie Lewis and he smells of Christmas cake.'

'Let me think for a minute,' Zoe said. She was getting into her stride now. 'I'm sure I've got something else to tell you,' she went on. 'Oh yeah. Did you hear about what happened in my Maths group, the other day?' She and Rebecca were in different groups for Maths. Zoe's group was definitely the liveliest.

'What?'

'Well you know we have Ms Burton.'

'Go on.' Ms Burton was a figure of fun throughout the school because she was so ridiculously old-fashioned. Her clothes looked as though she bought them in a charity shop and she had grey hair which she always wore pinned up in a bun. No one had ever seen her with her hair down.

'Well Susan Kingsland put her hand up and said, "Miss, do you leave your hair in a bun when you go to bed?"'

'What did Ms Burton say?'

'She said, "Susan Kingsland, will you concentrate on your work and stop behaving like an infant."' Zoe managed a very good impersonation of Ms Burton's stuffy manner. 'And then Susan said, "I only asked because I was thinking of doing my hair in the same way." So Ms Burton put her out of the class.'

'Typical Susan Kingsland,' Rebecca said.

'Wait,' Zoe said. 'That's not the end. After about ten minutes Ms Burton told me to open the door and tell her that she could come back in, which I did. But when she came in she'd done her hair up in this mad sort of bun.'

Zoe began laughing at the memory and Rebecca found herself joining in. Soon they were both helpless with laugher.

Every time one of them stopped, the other would start. At last the laughter died down of its own accord.

'Are you doing anything this evening?' Zoe asked, when she had calmed down sufficiently to talk.

Rebecca shook her head. She had not thought about 'doing something in the evening' for such a long time that she could hardly remember what it meant.

'There's a party tonight, if you want to come,' Zoe said. 'It's one of Jamie's friends.'

'No thanks,' Rebecca replied immediately. Laughter was one thing, but a party was something else altogether. It would be a long time yet before she would be ready for that.

'There might be some nice boys,' Zoe said.

'I'm sure there will be,' Rebecca said. 'I'm just a bit tired.'

She had originally intended to call in on Zoe for about half an hour but in the end she stayed for over two hours. It was strange sitting in Zoe's bedroom gossiping about school and boys. Sometimes she forgot herself and joined in whole-heartedly but other times she felt as if she were two people, one talking and laughing, the other observing the whole thing with complete detachment. It was as if the Rebecca that Zoe knew was someone she had once been and could only partially remember.

All the same it felt truly good to relax. She hadn't listened to music for weeks and weeks and there was a lot to catch up on. As usual, Zoe had all the latest and best recordings. She showed Rebecca the ones she had bought most recently. 'Listen to this one,' she said. 'It's really beautiful.' She took a CD out of its plastic case and put it in the player. There was a pause and then the music began.

Zoe generally liked music with a fierce, compulsive beat, but this track was different. It was soft and slow. There was something trance-like about the simple tune and the way it kept repeating. It seemed to penetrate right into Rebecca's soul, stirring up emotions in a way that was almost painful.

Rebecca let herself sink deeper and deeper into the music. A memory began drifting to the surface of her mind from when she was very little. She was seven years old. It was the coldest winter she had ever known. The world had been roofed in by iron-grey clouds for days on end. Then one morning she had got out of bed to find snow covering the ground in deep piles and drifts. She had squealed with excitement, then dressed herself as quickly as possible and rushed out of doors to make a snowman in the garden.

But after only a little while the cold had been too much for her and she had come back in tears, holding out her frozen fingers. Her mother had made her put her hands in a bowl of warm water to get the circulation back and at first that had been a relief. But as the blood began to pump back into her fingers they had started to hurt more than ever and she had cried out loud in dismay.

That was how she felt now, too. A part of her was coming back to life and she was not sure she was ready to deal with it just yet.

The music began to grow quieter and quieter. At last it died away altogether. 'Wasn't that brilliant?' Zoe asked.

Rebecca nodded. 'It was lovely,' she said.

'There's another track you've got to hear,' Zoe went on but Rebecca was already standing up.

'I've got to go,' she said.

Zoe looked disappointed. 'Do you really?' she asked.

'Mum will be expecting me back for dinner,' she said. 'It's been really nice, though,' she added.

Zoe stood up and followed Rebecca down to the front door. 'Sure you don't fancy going to the party tonight?' she asked.

'No thanks.'

'If you change your mind give us a ring.'

'I will.'

The two girls stood in the doorway and hugged each other.

'It was really good to see you,' Zoe said.

'Thanks. It was good to see you too,' Rebecca said. And as she turned and walked out of Zoe's house she knew that she really meant it.

CHAPTER SEVENTEEN

Christmas was coming. Rebecca spotted the first cardboard Santa Claus in the shops on the 23rd October. She told her mother about it.

'It gets earlier every year,' Carol complained.

They had both been dreading Christmas. It would be their first one without Richard. But now that Christmas fever had started, there was no getting away from it. From the very beginning of November the shops began stocking novelty gift items like Santa Claus boxer shorts and reindeer socks. Even the stallholders in the market where Rebecca caught the bus to school each morning had stopped selling their usual range of fruit and vegetables and cheap clothes. Instead they held out bundles of wrapping paper, tinsel and decorations. Radios everywhere were playing Christmas music. On the television people began to talk about how Christmas was a time for families to get together.

That hurt, the constant talk about families, about mothers and fathers and children. It was like walking along the road with a nail sticking into your foot. With every step the nail dug in a little deeper.

One day near the end of term Rebecca came back from

school to find her mother sitting at the kitchen table writing Christmas cards. 'Not you too!' she complained.

'We have to send out cards,' Carol said.

'Why?'

'Because people have been very kind to us. Anyway it's important to keep in touch.'

'I suppose so,' Rebecca agreed reluctantly. She got herself a drink of orange juice from the fridge and sat down next to Carol. 'I wish I lived on a planet where Christmas had never been invented,' she went on.

'They would have something else.'

Rebecca wasn't sure she agreed with this but she didn't feel like arguing.

'There's something I wanted to say,' Carol announced.

Rebecca put her drink down and waited. She knew that whenever her mother began like this, something important was coming.

'It's about the Christmas cards,' Carol went on, 'the ones we get. There are bound to be some with your father's name on, people who didn't hear about the accident, for one reason or another. You mustn't let it upset you.'

Rebecca nodded. She had been worried that her mother was going to say something much worse than this. Ever since the accident there had been a series of minor crises, starting with the missing insurance document – which had eventually turned up in a drawer at her father's work – including problems with bank accounts, the mortgage and the repayments on the car. But one by one her mother had straightened all of these out. Now it seemed, the only problems that remained were emotional ones.

Unfortunately, they could not be cleared up quite so easily.

Carol was looking earnestly at her and Rebecca realised that she wanted an answer. 'That's OK,' she said. 'I won't let it upset me.'

'Good.' Carol finished writing another card, put it in an envelope and addressed it. 'Would you like to stick on the stamps?' she suggested.

'OK.'

Carol handed her a sheet of stamps and she began tearing them off and sticking them on the envelopes which Carol had already addressed.

'Your grandfather phoned today,' Carol went on. 'He wondered if we'd like to spend Christmas with them.'

Rebecca experienced a sinking feeling when she heard this. 'What did you say?' she asked anxiously.

'I said I'd talk about it with you. What do you think?'

'Do we have to?'

Carol shook her head. 'No we don't,' she said. 'It just might be a bit hard, you know, only the two of us.'

'I don't care,' Rebecca said. She could just imagine what Christmas would be like with her mother's parents. There would be plenty of everything, too much probably, but everything would have to be just right. They were extremely conventional people. Meal times with them were always an elaborate ritual in which everyone was required to use the right knives and forks, say the right things, do everything in the right order. 'Can't we just have a quiet Christmas by ourselves?'

'OK,' Carol said. 'I just thought it was only fair to ask you. Don't worry, I'll phone them up tomorrow and say no thanks.'

Rebecca breathed a sigh of relief.

That was not the only invitation they received. Alan, who always had her father's parents for Christmas dinner, wanted them to spend Christmas Day with him. 'You can't spend the whole day on your own,' he told them, and in the end they agreed to go over there in the evening.

It was easier to turn down Father Maurice who rang up and suggested they might like to come to a special dinner which he was arranging for people who couldn't be with their loved ones at Christmas. Carol thanked him but declined, politely but firmly.

School began to wind down. They weren't doing much work now, just killing time until the end of term. Everyone was too full of Christmas to concentrate on anything. There was a tradition in Rebecca's school that each year at this time their form teacher, Ms Waddell, set up a mailbox in the classroom for the pupils to send each other cards. They had been doing this ever since they arrived at the school. They even used the same mailbox, wrapped in red shiny paper and decorated with cottonwool snow.

Everybody felt that the whole thing was getting a bit corny by now, but as the last week arrived they still found themselves writing cards to their friends and posting them in the mailbox. Even Rebecca found herself posting cards to Zoe and Hannah.

On the last day, just before they all finally left to go home, Ms Waddell opened up the mailbox and handed out the cards. Normally Rebecca got two or three cards but this year Ms Waddell handed her a huge bundle. Rebecca looked at them in surprise. There seemed to be one from every pupil in the class. She realised immediately that Ms Waddell must have told them to do it. All the same she felt suddenly touched by the gesture. She could feel her eyes filling up with tears. It was the unexpectedness of it. She swallowed hard and just about managed to say, 'Thanks, Miss.'

Ms Waddell smiled. 'Happy Christmas, Rebecca,' she said.

When she got home from school Rebecca found Carol standing next to the step-ladder on the upstairs landing.

'What are you doing, Mum?' she asked.

'Trying to make up my mind,' Carol said.

'About what?'

'About the decorations.' She explained that she had got out the step-ladder to go up into the loft where they kept the Christmas decorations, but then she had changed her mind. 'I'm not sure I really want to put up decorations this year,' she said. 'What do you think?'

Rebecca had been about to say that she would like the decorations up. The unexpected bundle of Christmas cards she had received had changed her mind about Christmas. For the first time since she had seen that cardboard Santa Claus in the department store nearly two months ago, she felt that Christmas was worth celebrating. On the way home she had been thinking about how she and Carol had always decorated the Christmas tree together every year. She had been looking forward to doing it again this time.

But one look at her mother's face changed her mind. She could see that her mother was close to tears. Rebecca was taken aback. For such a long time now her mother had been strong. She had dealt with everything that she had to. But suddenly the small matter of Christmas decorations threatened to throw her completely out of equilibrium.

'Let's not bother,' Rebecca said.

Carol looked relieved. 'Do you really feel that?' she asked.

'Really,' Rebecca told her.

'OK then,' Carol said, smiling. 'I'd better put this step-ladder away.'

Two days before Christmas it grew very cold. Carol and Rebecca were sitting in the lounge watching the television. The weather man had just predicted the possibility of snow in high places and her mother was groaning at the thought when there was a knock on the door.

'Is that someone for you?' Carol asked.

'I don't think so,' Rebecca said. She went to the door and opened it. Ben was standing there. She opened her mouth but could not speak. The cold air rushed past her into the house while she stood and stared.

'Hi,' he said.

Carol came out into the hall. 'Ben,' she said. 'I didn't know you were coming home for Christmas.'

'Neither did I,' he said.

'Well come in,' she told him.

Ben came inside and Rebecca shut the door behind him. They all went into the kitchen.

'Sit down,' Carol said. 'You look tired.' It was true. He did look tired and thinner than he had done. But he was still clean-shaven and there was something different about him. Rebecca was not sure what it was.

'Would you like a cup of coffee?' Carol asked.

'He doesn't drink coffee,' Rebecca said. She remembered

140

what a fuss he had made last time, insisting on drinking only herbal tea.

'I'd love a cup,' Ben said.

'What's happened to you?' Rebecca asked.

'I've just changed my mind about a few things,' Ben said.

'What sort of things?' Rebecca asked.

'Rebecca, he's just got in,' Carol said. 'Don't grill him.' She filled the kettle with water and put it on to boil. 'Did you have a good journey?' she asked.

'It took a long time,' Ben said. 'There were a lot of delays.'

The kettle came to the boil. Carol spooned instant coffee into a mug, filled it with water and topped it up with milk. She put the mug down in front of Ben. 'Well it's wonderful to see you again,' she told him.

'Thanks.' He held the cup in his hands and looked at its contents nervously, as if he was almost frightened to drink it.

'It won't poison you, you know,' Carol said.

He smiled. 'I know that.'

'So how long are you back for?' Rebecca asked. She could not contain her impatience any longer.

Ben sipped the coffee. Then he looked at them both. 'I don't know,' he said. 'For a while, if that's OK.' That was what was different about him, Rebecca realised: he looked nervous, unsure of himself, as if he no longer knew the answers to everything.

'Of course it's OK,' Carol said.

'It's just until I get myself sorted out.'

'What about Sat Sang?' Rebecca asked him.

'I'm finished with them.'

'How come?' she said. 'I thought you were on your way to enlightenment.'

'So did I. But I was wrong.'

Carol went over and hugged him. 'It's great to have you back,' she said. 'Stay as long as you like.'

'So we don't have to call you Krishna Devi any more?' Rebecca asked.

'No.'

'That's a relief anyway.'

'Are you sure it's OK – about me staying, I mean?' Ben asked.

'Of course it's OK,' Carol told him. 'This is your home. It's good to have you back. Isn't that right, Rebecca?'

Rebecca grinned at him. 'That's right,' she said. 'Welcome back to earth, spaceman.'

The next morning, straight after breakfast, Carol went out without telling them where she was going. Rebecca and Ben cleared up in the kitchen together. Ben was still not very talkative but at least he had lost that self-satisfied manner that had so infuriated Rebecca.

'So what made you see the light?' she asked him after they had put the dirty bowls and mugs in the dishwasher.

'I just started to look at things differently,' he replied.

'Yeah but what made you?' she insisted.

'Dad's death, I suppose. It just changed everything. I mean that sounds obvious. But it made me see the whole world differently. You know?'

'Absolutely.' Rebecca thought for a second of telling him about Maggie but she dismissed the idea immediately. He looked like he'd lost enough illusions without that. It was strange to think that by protecting him from this knowledge she was acting the role of the older child. She sniffed and twitched her nose.

'Have you got a cold?' Ben asked.

She shook her head. 'It's just a nervous habit,' she said. She surprised herself by saying that. It was the first time she had admitted it to anyone.

Ben nodded. He seemed to understand entirely. 'It's the stress,' he said. 'It hit me pretty hard, too.'

'Really?' She had somehow assumed that Ben had coped with their father's death without any obvious side-effects, other than losing his faith in Sat Sang.

'I had a lot of trouble sleeping,' he told her. 'I kept getting nightmares.'

'What sort of nightmares?'

'Really horrible ones. It was like I was in the car crash with Dad.' Ben looked as if he could hardly bear to talk about this but he went on. 'In the dream it was all my fault. I was arguing with Dad about Sat Sang. He was trying to tell me it was a waste of time and I was telling him he didn't know anything about it and he took his eye off the road and that was why he crashed.' As he spoke he stared at Rebecca out of haunted eyes.

'Well it wasn't your fault,' she told him. 'It wasn't anyone's. Not yours, not mine, not Mum's, not even Dad's. It was just an accident.'

'I know that,' Ben said. 'The thing is, afterwards, when I woke up, I couldn't get out of my mind the idea that he was right. That it was all a waste of time.'

Just then the front door opened and they heard Carol's voice. 'Can someone give me a hand?' she called. They both went out into the hall to find her carrying the most enormous Christmas tree. 'It was all they had left,' she told them. 'And now I can't get it through the door.'

But they did get it through, after a bit of a struggle. Then Ben found a bucket and filled it with earth from the garden. They placed the tree in the bucket, carried it into the middle of the lounge and stood back to admire it.

'Do you think it's too big?' Carol asked.

'I think it's wonderful,' Rebecca told her.

Then Carol got out the step-ladder she had put away a few days earlier and brought the decorations down from the loft. One by one they took them out and hung them on the tree: the glass balls, the wooden ornaments, the silver tinsel and last of all the fairy lights. Carol plugged them in and switched them on.

'It's beautiful,' Rebecca said. And it was, as beautiful as the Christmas trees she remembered from when she was a very little girl.

They were silent now, the three of them, for there was nothing left to say. Carol put one arm around Rebecca and the other around Ben. They stood there in the gathering darkness on the night before Christmas watching as the lights on the tree flashed on and off and the hardest year they had ever known moved inevitably towards its close. Somewhere hidden in its heart was the promise of spring. Not tomorrow or the day after but some day soon, the winter would pass, new growth would cover the bare earth and the bitter taste of grief would at last begin to fade.